The Rise of Annie Lone

A Novel

Charles Malone

ISBN: 0988333805
ISBN-13: 978-0-9883338-0-2

DEDICATION

For Barbara Malone, you taught me to be strong. For Mary Malone, you saw my potential and pushed me to live up to it.

Charles Malone

ACKNOWLEDGMENTS

Thank you Tanya Nozawa for helping me with your fantastic designing skills. Thank you Barbara Parry for encouraging me to try writing in the first place and pulling the bee stinger out of my neck.

CHAPTER 1

The door slammed at twenty minutes past two in the morning. Billy had just returned from yet another night out at the country club drinking with his friends. He threw his car keys onto the kitchen counter and undressed as he stumbled his way up the stairs toward the bedroom. Billy was still seething with anger from what he had heard that night.

Having heard the door open, Annie stayed in bed hoping that this would be one of those nights that Billy would come in and simply pass out on the couch. As the bedroom door swung open and Billy entered the room, she quickly realized that she wouldn't be so lucky. She knew that he had slightly sobered up before leaving the country club because of the tone of his voice. She knew that he intended to have his way with her as he had done on many occasions before.

"Annie! Annie! Don't pretend to be asleep!" called out Billy. He climbed onto the bed and started tugging at Annie's pajamas while simultaneously trying to roll her over onto her back. Annie finally gave in and rolled over. With a sinking feeling, she realized that this was going to be one of those nights. Two years into their four year marriage, Billy had started forcing himself onto her. Most of the time he would come home so drunk that he was thwarted by his inability to get an erection but this was not always the case.

The first time it happened Annie had attempted to resist but Billy choked her until she passed out. When she woke up he had violently raped her, breaking the sacred trust between a husband and a wife. Her tears were unrelenting. Some were caused by the pain she felt as her whole body ached. She had bruises on her inner thighs, ankles, and arms. Annie's back felt like it had been twisted. She also cried because the man she loved had done the unthinkable. As Billy lay next to her snoring in a drunken stupor, Annie thought about what she should do. She did have options. She could call 911. She could gather up her belongings and leave. She could do both. As she started to get up to clean herself, Billy awoke.

"Where are you going? Lay your ass down. Don't even think of trying to leave me. I'll see you in hell before I let that happen. You're my woman and don't ever fucking forget that. I am tired of tip-toeing around here waiting for you to decide when to screw me. I work hard to take care of this family and damn it I deserve some fucking consideration," declared Billy.

Bewildered by the sudden change in Billy and frightened at the prospect of him hurting her anymore, Annie laid back down. Since then, Annie had endured this humiliation, pain, and degradation on numerous occasions. Occasionally, Billy would rough her up with some shoving, pushing, and slapping to let her know he was in command but nothing that permanently injured her. However, tonight was different.

"James Midkiff told me that he saw you at the grocery store."

"Yes, James said hi," Annie said as she rolled over onto her side facing Billy.

"He said that you were really *friendly*. He also said that you looked great. Did I tell you to look good for other motherfuckers, especially that motherfucker James Midkiff?" Billy said in an angry tone. "No, bitch, I didn't. You're going to learn that I own you."

Realizing how angry he was about her talking to Jimmy, Annie tried to get up off the bed to calm him down but Billy pushed her back down. James Midkiff had been the managing partner at Billy's old law firm. Billy hated James because he went around bragging about winning large jury verdicts for his clients. James never gave credit to the junior or senior associates who helped him put the case together for trial.

Most of all, however, Billy hated James for the way he looked at the associate attorneys' wives at firm-sponsored events. James never made any comments about the associates' wives but it was widely circulated in the rumor mill that he had hit on and even slept with some of them. Hearing James' comment about Annie drove Billy crazy. Billy avoided confronting James primarily out of fear. The fear that it would adversely affect his legal career if he said something to him as James had wide connections throughout the legal community that could result in Billy being blackballed. So rather than confronting

James, Billy chose to come home and take his anger out on Annie.

"I was just being polite to Jimmy. Nothing happened," said Annie.

"Shut the fuck up. I'm going to give you just what you're looking for," yelled Billy. He began to tug at Annie's panties as she struggled to get up. As he tore her panties off, Billy said "look at how wet you are just at the mention of old Jimmy." He climbed atop Annie and started forcing her knees apart.

"Billy, don't do this."

"You don't get to tell me what to do," As he attempted to insert his cock into her. "Just knowing how turned on you are for old Jimmy pisses me off. You belong to me bitch and when I'm done you'll know it." He continued trying to force himself into her but was unable to get an erection. Billy got off of Annie and went to the bathroom.

"Don't move bitch."

Annie thought to herself she should get the hell out of there but was paralyzed by fear. Her legs and arms wouldn't work. Before she could do anything, Billy yelled, "I got what you want." When Billy returned he had a toilet plunger in his hand.

"I'm not going to disappoint you tonight. You want a hard stiff one, right? Well, here it is." Annie jumped off the bed and tried to run out of the room. Billy grabbed her by the hair and threw her back onto the bed.

"Get back on that fucking bed. Let's pretend this is good old Jimmy," Billy said as he grabbed her by the hair and threw her back onto the bed. He then climbed on top of her and held her down. Annie tried to push Billy off of her but his 6'3" 195 pound frame was too much for her. Annoyed by her attempts to get out from under him, Billy punched her in the nose and eye with two quick but hard blows. Annie was severely dazed by the blows. Then an excruciating pain set in as if a horse had kicked her in the face. Brushing her hand across her face, she realized that her eye socket and nose may be broken.

Billy inserted the plunger handle into her vagina and forcefully shoved it into her over and over again. The pain was unbearable. As Annie lost consciousness, she heard Billy say, "This *is* what you wanted. Old Jimmy will satisfy you."

CHAPTER 2

Annie awoke to the sound of nine-month old Julia crying and looked at the clock next to the bed which read 4:45 in the morning. As she started to move she felt agonizing pain, but her baby needed her so she had to get up to see what the baby girl needed. Not only did her eye and nose feel as if they had been smashed but her vagina throbbed with a pain that reverberated throughout her body. Next to her, Billy was sprawled out all over the bed and completely still with a nearly empty bottle of vodka under his arm.

This had been the worst assault Billy had perpetrated against her since he had begun beating and raping her almost two years ago. She couldn't understand how the man who had once professed undying love for her could cause her so much pain. She was at a loss for why Billy turned from being a sweet and loving man to a brutal monster. Tonight, she thought to herself, she needed to forget about the past and think about the future. That meant she had to get away from Billy but she was so scared. He had already warned her that he would kill her if she tried to leave and, with what happened tonight, she believed him.

Annie got Julia out of her crib and carried her downstairs to the kitchen where she got out a thermometer and took her temperature, which came back as 102 degrees. After giving her some infant acetaminophen to lower her temperature, Annie sat down on the couch with her daughter and a bottle to get her back to sleep and remembered how wonderful things were when she and Billy first married. Billy treated her like a princess. He always opened doors for her. He was very attentive to her needs and desires. He even gave her foot massages and Annie didn't let just anyone touch her feet.

Annie was very self-conscious about her feet. Though she stood 5'8" tall as a woman, she wore a size twelve in men's shoes, which made it nearly impossible for her to find cute footwear made for a woman. As a result, she had always made efforts to hide her feet from the world; especially would-be boyfriends. But she let her guard down and allowed Billy to touch her feet. It had been a whirlwind love affair between the two of them.

But she also noticed some signs. Once at a dinner party, Billy's brother complemented Annie on the light blue spaghetti strap dress she wore. Billy crushed a glass in his bare-hand though he never said a word to Annie or his brother. Everyone at the party rushed to help stop the bleeding. He pretended that it was merely an accident but Annie wondered about his response because she noticed the look on his mother's and brother's faces. They looked as if they had seen Billy act this way before. But she pushed that to the back of her mind. She gave Billy the benefit of the doubt. Besides he had been nothing but a gentleman to her the whole time. But in hindsight she now remembered that Billy didn't talk to his brother for nearly a year after that comment.

Billy was also an ultra-competitive man she recalled. He had to win at everything. Whether it was on the basketball court, in the courtroom, or in an argument with his friends, Billy consistently sought to be in the vanguard of everything he did. Ambition was his other constant. This ambition had driven him to heavy drinking as the toll of working in a law firm where he didn't get much recognition for his hard work and passed over for partner several times despite turning in top notch performances in exceeding billable hour requirements and winning several high profile cases. Billy's unremitting ambition coupled with his drinking and disappointment with the direction of his career had driven him to hurting the woman he once swore to love.

Sitting holding a fast asleep Julia, Annie made her decision. Billy didn't love her anymore. Billy had caused her immense emotional and physical pain. She needed to separate herself from him. Annie took Julia back to her bedroom and put her in her crib. She called her mother when she returned downstairs. She had a plan.

"Mom, I need help. I need you to come and pickup Julia and take her to a hotel with you. I'm leaving Billy and I know he'll flip out and try to threaten me. I don't want her to be here when this happens."

Annie's mother, Daryn Mallory, asked, "What happened?"

"Billy accused me of coming on to James Midkiff."

"Annie, did he do it again. You have to call the police. The law is on your side now-a-days," said her mother.

"I don't want to ruin his career."

"To hell with his career, Annie! You need to think about your life and that you need to be around to take care of Julia."

"Don't worry about that mom. Just say you'll do it and come pick her up now before Billy wakes up."

"Okay, I'm on my way."

Daryn understood all to well the pain and suffering that Annie was experiencing. Daryn had suffered from the same type of abuse for decades at the hands of Annie's father. Annie's father beat Daryn once a week for nearly thirty-five years until he had a stroke and couldn't do it anymore. Even then, he belittled Daryn on a daily basis. On a few occasions, neighbors called the police but, without exception, the police never did anything to protect her. In fact, in those days, police never intervened to protect the victim because it was considered a private family matter when a man was *correcting* the mistakes of his wife. Daryn's nightmare of verbal and physical assaults didn't end until he died of a massive heart attack.

CHAPTER 3

Seeing the car pull into the driveway, Annie ran outside to meet her mother with Julia and a bag of Julia's clothes and food. After a big hug and kiss, Annie handed Julia over to her mother to grab Julia's car seat out of the car. In shock at the sight of her daughter, Daryn said, "Annie, you have dried blood all over your face and legs. What did he do to you?"

"Mom, just take care of Julia and get out of here before he wakes up."

"I love you Annie," said Daryn.

"I love you too mom. Now get the hell out of here."

After her mother pulled out of the driveway, Annie turned her attention to the open front door and started slowly making her way back toward it. She knew that she faced a horrible monster inside. She wondered how to tell him that she was going to leave him. She thought that it might be safer to call the police and have them present when she told Billy that she was done with this pain. The monster that was Billy Lone had previously left Annie with bruises and scratches on various parts of her body as well as countless other injuries as a result of the violent rapes he had perpetrated against her.

But police involvement could lead to Billy being charged and convicted of a felony for the assault and rape that he had perpetrated against her that night, which could lead to his disbarment and the end of his career. She didn't want to hurt him in that way. All that she really wanted was for Billy to stop beating her. More importantly, she wanted Billy to leave her and Julia alone. Her fear was that Billy would simply refuse both requests.

But she had made up her mind. Annie intended on confronting Billy and giving him an ultimatum. As she slowly moved back into the house, she remembered where Billy kept the .38 handgun and the bullets. Annie thought that if she had the gun she could use it to discourage Billy from attacking her during the confrontation. She retrieved it from the gun safe in the garage. With the gun in hand, Annie slowly walked up the stairs toward the bedroom. After reaching the door, Annie slowly pushed it open and looked into the room. It was too dark to see if Billy was still on the bed. She slowly raised her hand pointing the gun into the room. Taking slow and cautious steps Annie crossed the threshold. As she entered the room, Billy stepped from behind the door and punched her in the face knocking her unconscious.

Annie began to regain consciousness while lying on the hallway floor. "What the fuck are you doing with my gun?" Billy said while sitting on the bed holding the gun he'd taken from Annie. She was sprawled on the hallway floor with her feet just inside the doorway dazed from the powerful blow Billy had used to subdue her.

"Billy, we can't continue this way," said Annie trying to shack the cobwebs from her head and focus.

"Continue what way? What are you talking about? If you're talking about leaving, you can forget that shit because I'll fucking kill you first. You ever come at me with a gun again bitch there'll be hell to pay. Have you checked on Julia this morning yet? If not, get your ass up and get in there and take care of my baby." Billy grabbed Annie by the hair and dragged her down the hallway to Julia's nursery. As he opened the door, he saw that the crib was empty.

"Where the fuck is Julia?" Annie didn't say a word, which angered Billy.

"Where is she? Is she with your mother? Well, we're going to go pick her up. Get your ass in the shower and get that damned blood off of yourself so that we can go in public."

A completely terrified Annie crawled down the hallway toward the bathroom as Billy walked down the stairs glaring at her over his shoulder with an angry expression on his face. Nothing about the confrontation had gone the way she had planned it. She felt absolutely hopeless. Billy didn't care about her anymore. He didn't hesitate to inflict severe injuries to her. This was the last straw. Finally, crawling into the bathroom and pushing the door shut, Annie accepted the fact that she'd have to call the police. Since he had the gun, she'd have to wait because she believed that at this very moment he'd probably use it on her.

After she got out of the shower, Annie went downstairs and discovered Billy had passed out yet again on the couch in the family room. This time he had a half-empty bottle of rum lying in front of him. The bottle had been full the night before. But Billy's appetite for alcohol had grown exponentially over the past several years. He drank large quantities of any hard liquor he could get his hands on.

Seeing Billy sprawled out on the couch, a sense of excitement and opportunity grew in her. She was excited because Billy wouldn't be able to force her to go get Julia. She could end this now by packing everything and getting the hell out of there. But would it work? Simply leaving would only enrage Billy and he would set out on a journey to find her and Julia. He would go to the police and report that Annie had kidnapped Julia and accuse her of all sorts of bad things. Simply leaving probably wouldn't work. What should she do? With a sense of despair growing in her gut, Annie decided that the only way to get away from Billy would be to once and for all end it.

In a flash, Annie walked to the kitchen and got a butcher's knife. She walked back to the family room as if she were in a funeral procession. She wasn't a killer. But he would never leave her alone. He'd pursue her wherever she went. She had to do this. The love she felt for him had died long ago. She stood over Billy's drunken body, staring at his face. She recalled every time Billy ever hit her; every agonizing slap to the face or cruel shove. She thought of every time Billy brutally and uncaringly raped her like she was a piece of meat without any feeling. Without further hesitation she plunged the knife into Billy's chest. On the first impact, the knife slightly bent from hitting Billy's ribcage. His eyes sprang open immediately and he gasped for air. As quick as lightening, she thrust the knife into Billy three additional times as he wheezed his final breaths. Annie dropped the knife next to him. She collapsed onto the couch. With a feeling of relief and freedom overcoming her, Annie began to sob uncontrollably.

She sat there on the couch next to Billy's body for nearly an hour trying to decide what to do next. Before she could come up with a plan, Billy's friend, Gerald Stone, knocked on the door. Annie jumped to her feet and immediately froze as the front door was ajar. Without any warning, Gerald pushed the door open.

As the door swung open, Gerald called out for Billy. "Hey, Billy! Let's go man. We're going to be late." Seeing Billy's bloodied body lying on the couch, Gerald panicked. Looking at Annie, Gerald said, "What did you do? What happened here? I gotta get some help here for Billy."

"Gerald, he's already dead" said Annie. As Annie walked toward Gerald, he began to step backward toward the front door.

"You stay right there," said Gerald. "I'm calling the police." Annie stopped moving toward Gerald and, realizing that she had grabbed the knife when Gerald opened the door, dropped it to the floor as Gerald dialed 911 on his cell phone.

CHAPTER 4

After undergoing surgery on her face and vagina and spending nearly six weeks in Olympia General Hospital, Annie was transferred to the Thurston County Jail. This was not unexpected as her attorney, Sylvia Gray, had advised her that the Thurston County Prosecuting Attorney was seriously considering charging her with Murder in the First Degree, Murder in the Second Degree, and Manslaughter in the First Degree.

Indeed, the county prosecutor finally decided to bring charges against Annie for the death of Billy. The state's argument was simply that Annie had a chance to get away from Billy and should have done so as opposed to stabbing him to death. After attempts to reach a plea deal failed, Sylvia formally filed to raise the defenses of Justifiable Use of Force and Battered Woman's Syndrome (BWS). Sylvia used the Justifiable Use of Force defense on the grounds that Billy had severely beaten, raped, and tortured Annie that night and his torturous campaign against her never really ceased. The BWS defense was based on the two years of physical and sexual abuse Annie suffered at the hands of her husband, which left her no choice.

On her first day in the county jail (the same day she filed Annie's formal defense pleadings), Annie met with Sylvia even before she was assigned a cell because Sylvia wanted to take action quickly and didn't want to waive Annie's constitutional right to a speedy trial, which had to take place within sixty days after the arraignment under the state Superior Court Criminal Rules. She didn't want to give the prosecution too much time to turn a weak case against Annie into a strong case by concocting some crazy motive-based tale that they would tell the jury. She knew that Annie's best chance rested with her story of being abused and assaulted for years.

"I had to do it. I couldn't stop him from coming after me and Julia. Don't they understand that?" said Annie.

Sylvia began, "Calm down Annie. We have to decide what to do at this point. The evidence gathered at your house clearly points to your guilt."

"I understand that but I didn't have a choice. I want a jury to hear my story," Annie said as her voice began to crack. "I'm not going to plead guilty to second degree Murder when I couldn't stop him from coming after me."

"First things first. I think there is plenty of evidence to support your defenses. We simply have to gather it. If we're going to go with the Battered Woman's Syndrome defense, we have to get you evaluated by a mental health professional as well as gather all of your medical records to illustrate the savagery of the abuse you endured in your marriage. I'll have my paralegal draft a release for you to sign giving me permission to access all of your medical history and get it delivered to you."

"What should I do?" inquired Annie.

"Nothing! Sit tight. Let me get the ball rolling on putting together your defense. I'll keep you in the loop as things progress. Do you have anymore questions for me?"

"No. I just want to tell my story."

"I'll see to it that you get your chance. Hang in there Annie. I'll be in touch." As Sylvia exited the interview room, Annie sat nervously waiting to be taken to her cell.

CHAPTER 5

After meeting with Sylvia, a female Corrections and Custody Officer (CO) walked Annie back to her cell where she would spend her first night since arriving at the Thurston County Jail. She arrived at the cell and the CO escorting her handed Annie a small bag of some personal items and toiletries along with a pair of shoes. Once they reached the cell front, the CO yelled to the CO in the control booth, "open cell 15." The CO noticed Annie wiping tears from her eyes.

"Do you need to talk to the mental health counselor?" asked the CO.

Annie answered, "No."

"Well, you can always yell to the officer if you change your mind," said the CO.

"Thanks. I do need something else. These shoes here in the bag aren't going to fit."

"They should..." the CO paused when she looked at Annie's unusually large feet. "What size you need?"

The now self-conscious Annie tried to hide her feet and softly replied, "Size 12 in a men's shoe."

"Close cell 15," shouted the CO. "I'll get those for you."

In a low whisper the CO said, "Good luck! I hope you beat this thing. I was in a relationship like that and if it hadn't been for my brother I probably would be dead," as she took the cuffs off of Annie. Annie looked back at the CO with a surprised look on her face as she walked into her cell. She could see the look of concern on the face of the CO. Though these were mere words Annie gathered some solace and strength from them that helped her center herself and get prepared for the first of many nights being caged like an animal.

The cell was poorly lit and smelled like a mix of urine and bleach because the inmate porters generally did a poor job cleaning. Annie noticed that the top bunk was occupied by another person covered nearly entirely under a blanket. She worried that the occupant of the bunk was some deranged drug addict or maybe a child murderer. What would she say to the woman? What if she wanted to fight? She tried to get her thoughts under control. She didn't want her fear of the unknown to turn her into a paranoid wreck. This was her first time in a jail cell. Realizing that she hadn't a clue about acceptable conversation or actions in jail, Annie decided to be on guard for anything. Annie was a law-abiding person with no experience in these sorts of things. She had never even gotten a speeding ticket in her life. Now, here she was locked up in the county jail unable to hug and kiss Julia. Unable to move on after the last two tumultuous years of her life, she thought of the predicament she was now in.

Annie began to go through the items the jailers allowed her to bring into the cell. She pulled out her toothbrush, toothpaste, deodorant, and some other feminine toiletries. However, in the bottom of the bag Annie found a surprise. It was a letter from the president of the Women's Alliance for Battered Women (WABW). She noticed that this letter had a personal touch with a real signature rather than the traditional signature stamp used by large organizations. The letter said,

"Dear Annie, we are a nonprofit organization that raises awareness about the amount of domestic violence that still goes on in society today through a strong public relations apparatus and a political unit that engages elected officials nationwide. We also have a legal division that provides resources to women who face criminal charges in connection with personal relationships where the women have been victims of domestic violence.

We evaluate each case and decide if the woman suffers from

Battered Woman's Syndrome (BWS).
This is done with the assistance of one
of our trusted licensed psychologists. If
the conclusion is that you suffer from
BWS, we will provide you with a list of
available attorneys with expertise in the
area of arguing BWS as a defense. You
may choose any attorney from that list
and our organization will pay for your
attorney fees and costs. However, this
usual process does not apply to you.

As your current attorney Sylvia
Gray is also a licensed psychiatrist and a
member of our board of directors, she
indicated that her discussions with you
over the last several weeks while you
convalesced in the hospital has led her
to believe that you suffer from BWS.
Based on her diagnosis we have decided
to pay the costs of your defense.

You are not alone in your
struggle. Many of us women who serve
on the staff of the WABW have also
been victims of domestic violence. We
understand the pain you went through
and the uncertain future you face. We
will stand with you in your time of need.
Please to do not hesitate to contact us
even if you simply just want someone to

talk to."

Annie felt a swelling of appreciation and relief that the WABW had decided to assist her in fighting the state's prosecution of this unjust case against her at Sylvia's request. In the six weeks since Sylvia had been representing Annie, she had never mentioned that she was a member of such an important organization. Perhaps she didn't want to get Annie's hopes up about the WABW providing her with assistance. Nevertheless, this was positive news that gave Annie some respite from the quandary she faced. She had made her decision to turn down the state's plea deal. Now it was time to fight the allegations that she "murdered" Billy.

Annie sincerely felt that she had killed her husband in self-defense or, as the state of Washington calls it, it was justifiable homicide. Billy had made it clear that Annie was *his* and no one else's and that if she tried to leave him there would be painful consequences. Sitting in the jail cell her mind wandered back to those horrific thoughts. Annie spent many nights crying in the bathroom, hallway, or some room out of Billy's sight after he had brutally imposed his will on her with forced sexual acts or slapping her around for sport. She couldn't wrap her head around how the man she loved could possibly go there. Especially when Annie had told him of her childhood; a childhood filled with sleepless nights of hearing her mother's violent assaults at the hands of her own father.

When she was young Annie would often just lie

there in fear as she heard her mother scream in agony from being punched in the face over and over again. The next day she would see her mother with blackened eyes, missing teeth, and bumps and scrapes to various parts of her body. When Annie got older she would often intervene in an effort to protect her mother. While her father never touched her in violence, the images of seeing him attack her mother scarred her. One such occasion stood out in her mind when she was sixteen years old.

She came home from a friend's house and discovered her father drunk, trying to load his gun in the living room. Luckily he was so inebriated that he couldn't steady his hand long enough to get any of the bullets into the firearm. Annie simply took the gun and bullets from her father. Her mother, Daryn, lay on the kitchen floor sobbing with a bloody lip as if she had surrendered to the fact that he was going to kill her. Daryn told Annie that she had told her father that the deep freezer had broken and all the meat in it had thawed and gone bad. Her father flipped out, blaming Daryn for the machine breaking down. Billy knew full well this and other experiences from her childhood adversely impacted her but he didn't seem to care. When Billy started hitting her he violated the trust she had placed in him.

While reading her letter, Annie hadn't noticed the still figure under the blanket on the top bunk had uncovered her head and was now looking at her.

"Hi! I'm Sibyl. Sibyl Enoch."

Annie glanced up and said, "I'm Annie Lone."

"I've heard of you. You killed your husband a few weeks ago. What for?" said a nonchalant Sibyl. Annie didn't respond. "I know. Every girl meets some guy at some point in her life who wants to show his control and ownership of us women. It's that damned 'caveman' syndrome. Somehow that 'caveman' is part of what draws us to these animals. Must be something in the DNA, you know, primal stuff. If it makes you feel better, I'm here because my fiancé used my apartment to hide his heroine stash. I told them that George led me to believe that he was a mortgage broker. I didn't even know that he was dealing the stuff but we were together for years and the detectives don't believe that I couldn't have known. Not to mention the fact that the son-of-a-bitch told the investigators that I was the 'brains behind the operation.' So, I'm facing drug possession with intent to distribute charges that could land me in prison for a long time. In all honesty, I had a forgery conviction five years ago for stealing my mother's checkbook and signing her name to two checks when I was using cocaine. I think the detectives are holding that against me even though I've been clean for the last five years and working full-time. Hell, I even got a degree from South Puget Sound Community College but I'm not catching any slack from these bastards," Sibyl breathlessly explained.

"Well, I have to get out of here to take care of my baby," Annie said in a concerned voice as she folded up the letter in her hand.

"Yeah, you don't want her to end up in foster care," quipped Sibyl.

"She won't. My mother will take care of her for

me until I get out of here."

Sibyl asked, "How old is your baby?"

"Julia's ten and a half months old," responded Annie. "She is my responsibility. She needs me."

"It could be awhile before you get out," said Sibyl.

"Don't say that. Don't ever say that to me," Annie spoke in a forceful tone because that was a potential reality that she didn't want to face. Even with the assistance of WABW, there was no guarantee that she would be able to overcome the prosecutor's barrage of allegations of premeditation and revenge.

"Well, you know that there are a lot of us girls out there pulling for you Annie."

"Serious?"

"Serious! All sorts of women's groups have been writing the prosecutor's office to complain about what they are doing to you."

"I saw them talking about me on the news a couple of times while I was in the hospital but I never saw much else. I spent much of the time out of it because of the pain medications they were giving me."

"It's an honor to meet the famous Annie Lone. It's almost lights out so goodnight. I need by beauty sleep," laughed Sibyl as she pulled her blanket up around her shoulders and turned toward the wall.

"Famous? I don't know about that but it's good to meet you too. Goodnight Sibyl."

With that Annie turned out her light and put her head on the small jail-issued pillow. She stared at the chipped paint and crumbling cinder block construction of her cell's gray wall as she contemplated the next steps of her life in front of a jury.

CHAPTER 6

Annie was filled with excitement as she awaited her mother's arrival for visitation. Today she would get to see her baby. For a loving mother to go a day without seeing her child is like a lifetime and Annie had spent six lifetimes without seeing her darling Julia. From a very early age, all that Annie knew was that she wanted to get married and have babies. That had been her calling. Yes, graduating from the prestigious Western Washington University summa cum laude with her Bachelor of Science in Chemistry had been one of her best achievements but, for Annie, having Julia was like winning a Nobel Prize. The little girl was the light in her life.

The CO who whispered the words of comfort had arrived at the cell front to secure and escort Annie for her visit with her mother and Julia. She yelled to the control booth, "Open cell 15!"

Annie noticed that her name tag had CO Wilson engraved into it. As the CO secured Annie in restraints for the trip to the visitation room, she asked her, "What's your first name?"

"Dee. How are you holding up in here?"

In an excited voice, Annie responded, "Ready to see my baby. It seemed like this day would never come."

As Annie and CO Wilson moved down the hallway, she walked at a quick pace toward the visitation room despite the restraints. She knew that she wouldn't be allowed to hold Julia but simply being able to see her filled Annie with excitement. Once they reached the visitation room entrance, CO Wilson removed the restraints from her wrists and, using her keys, opened the door allowing Annie to go in.

The sight of her ten and a half month old baby in her mother's arms made Annie immediately start crying with joy. Annie moved quickly to take a seat in front of the glass partition between herself and her mother and Julia. Picking up the phone receiver, Annie started, "Mom, thank you so much for bringing her here to see me. How's she doing?"

"She's doing great. She's too young to know what's going on. Don't you worry Annie. I'll take care of her until you get yourself out of here."

"I know you will Mom. The good news is that Sylvia is involved in an organization that helps women in my predicament – you know victims of domestic violence."

"Oh Annie, that's great news. What about getting me temporary custody of Julia while you're in here? I haven't heard anything from Billy's family but we should be ready for anything that may come."

"Great idea Mom! Next time I talk to Sylvia I'll ask her to also assist you in getting guardianship over her until I get out."

"What about your case? Are you still going ahead with the Battered Woman's Defense?"

"I don't have a choice," explained Annie, "the prosecutor will only accept a plea deal that puts me in here for twenty years. I can't possibly stay in here that long. I'll miss Julia growing up. I won't be there when she needs me the most. You know, the first time a boy breaks her heart, prom night pictures, or to help her pick out her first bra. So I have to fight this thing Mom."

"So long as you know, you have my full support Annie," Daryn exclaimed.

"I know Mom! Thank you for everything. I love you."

"I love you too Annie."

"Put the phone to Julia's ear. I want her to hear my voice."

"Okay."

"Hey baby girl. How's my baby girl? Momma will be out of here soon. I love you." Julia's eyes lit up at the sound of her mother's familiar voice. For the rest of the visit, Annie and Daryn talked about a few other mundane topics.

      After the visit with her family Annie felt rejuvenated. The visit had given her the strength she needed to face the jury next week. Her resiliency to fight the allegations lodged against her by the prosecutor had grown exponentially.

CHAPTER 7

Sylvia put on a great defense for Annie. Her medical records showed, and her treating physicians from the Olympia General Hospital Emergency Room testified about, the innumerable injuries she suffered as a result of Billy's violent acts against her on that night as well as on prior occasions. Three of Billy's former girlfriends testified about his acts and statements of violence directed at them. Even more importantly, Annie's expert psychiatrist explained to the jury what Battered Woman Syndrome was and how it affected its victims. The expert had also testified about how Annie had been changed by Billy's abuse of her over the past two years. Sylvia drew a clear line between Billy's actions and Annie's response on the night he was killed.

However, not to be outdone, Deputy Prosecuting Attorney (DPA) Hetty Michele hammered Annie throughout the week-long trial. Michele argued that she had planned the murder of Billy by calling her mother to pick up Julia and getting Billy's gun. Michele conceded that Annie's plan failed because Billy successfully disarmed her but with that failure Annie improvised choosing as the murder weapon a knife while Billy was asleep. If things were that bad, argued the prosecutor, why had she not contacted the police. The prosecutor portrayed her as a woman who would do anything to get rid of her husband in order to keep their baby all to herself. The icing on the cake was the testimony of Gerald Stone about Annie advancing toward him with the knife still in her hand when he stopped by to pick up Billy.

Beyond the legal combat that took place between Sylvia Gray and the DPA Hetty Michele, the courtroom and courthouse steps had become a media circus during jury selection, the trial, and deliberations as domestic violence and women's organizations circled the wagons to support Annie. Television talking heads showed up and opined about the necessity of not having a double standard for women who kill men. Women's rights advocates advanced the notion that American society had always, until recently, had a double standard that allowed men to *discipline* wives who got out of line with minimal law enforcement involvement. After days of verbal sparring, the jury verdict had come in.

As the judge read the jury's decision of not guilty on the Murder in the First Degree charge, Annie was elated. Her hopes were soon dashed when the judge said guilty of Murder in the Second Degree, which the judge confirmed by polling the jury at the request of Sylvia. Her elation turned to pure despondency as she realized she faced a long prison stay and that Julia would grow-up without her after all. The rest of what the judge said had become nothing more than a mish-mash of garbled sound that was incomprehensible to her. All that Annie knew was that she would have to go to prison. What was she going to do? She couldn't live this way; locked in some prison cell away from the most important person in her life. Tears filled her eyes as she sobbed uncontrollably. Sylvia did her best to calm Annie but she became hysterical. Two Thurston County Jail COs advanced toward Annie in an effort to calm her down. "Annie, I need you to calm down, this is not the end of the world," said Sylvia herself a bit emotional as she whipped a tear from her cheek.

"It's the end of my world," retorted Annie. "I can't do this. I can't be separated from Julia. She's just a baby."

"You see those two COs. They are going to be coming to put shackles on you so don't panic. Please stay calm Annie. It's not the end of the world because I'll be filing an immediate motion asking the court to set aside the jury verdict and, if that fails, an appeal of the jury's verdict," Sylvia whispered. "Just let me do my job."

As Sylvia concluded, the two COs moved on either side of Annie and started applying restraints to her. After they escorted her back to her cell, she cried over and over again. The judge scheduled her sentencing for next week but she wanted to know now what her punishment would be. She couldn't sit in that cell rotting while the judge and prosecution planned her extended stay in state custody. But she had to wait.

Sibyl tried to comfort her. Sibyl lightened the mood by telling Annie funny stories from her past. She even offered to play card games and checkers with her but Annie was indifferent to all of these things. They didn't even get a full final week together. The next day, Thursday, the court sentenced Sibyl and on Friday a transport bus headed for the women's prison picked her up. Now Annie was all alone for the weekend and had to wait for Wednesday, sentencing day, to arrive. She became lost in her sorrow. As she lay on her bunk, she could only think about how she wouldn't be here had Billy simply treated her better. Why would any man treat a woman the way he treated her? She surely had done nothing to deserve what he had done to her.

That night Annie dreamed a vividly horrid nightmare; a nightmare where Julia grew up not knowing who her mother was. A nightmare where Julia fell in with the wrong group of individuals and wound up incarcerated in a state penitentiary. A nightmare where Julia, missing the love of a mother and a father, ended up with a man who never showed her any love but instead introduced her to hardcore drugs, how to sell her body, and how to *listen* to what her man said. Annie opened her eyes and sat straight up in her bunk. She was completely covered in sweat from head to toe, terrified by what she had just seen in her dream. Sentencing day couldn't arrive soon enough.

Even though Sylvia had argued for the low end of the sentencing range of just over 10 years because Annie's offender score was a 0 as she hadn't even had a traffic ticket, the prosecution requested the top of the sentencing range of 18 years and 4 months. The judge mindlessly followed the prosecution's recommendation sentencing Annie to 220 months in the custody of the state after having rejected Sylvia's motion to set aside the jury verdict as not supported by the evidence.

Now Annie knew her fate and had to ready herself to fight. She met once more with Sylvia and they decided that an appeal was definitely in order because Annie presented compelling evidence to support her justifiable homicide and BWS defense that had been ignored by the jury. Sylvia thought Annie's chances on appeal were pretty good. For now, she would have to start serving out her sentence.

CHAPTER 8

The Washington State Department of Corrections' bus left the Thurston County Jail promptly at 7 a.m. Friday with six newly convicted female felons. It was a relatively cold morning and many of the roads were slippery from the freezing fog that had developed overnight. The bus had several stops to make along the way north to pick up other state inmates from county jails. Annie sat in her seat shackled not only literally but figuratively. During the long ride Annie went over the trial in her head over and over again. She couldn't see where Sylvia did anything wrong. She couldn't see where any of the defense witnesses went wrong. They were exceedingly clear, accurate, and convincing but the jury didn't accept their testimony. Neither did they accept Annie's testimony.

She later learned that some of the jurors had participated in media interviews and expressed their opinion that they simply didn't believe what she had said. The jurors thought that Annie simply wanted to get rid of her husband for a variety of half-cooked up reasons. They believed that the ex-girlfriends' testimony was jaded and colored by the fact that they had broken up with Billy. After hours of obsessively mulling the trial over, Annie eventually dozed off. She would be arriving at her new home soon.

The Mount Baker Corrections Center for Women (MBCCW) in Whatcom County opened in 1978. It was designed to house 1,000 inmates but currently housed 1,215. Superintendent Sarah Loons and Associate Superintendent Jennifer Welch led the institution. Sarah had gained her national reputation for cleaning up Alabama's notoriously dangerous and dirty Tutwiler women's prison. MBCCW had earned a similarly notorious reputation but it was because of allegations of mistreatment of mentally ill inmates and inadequate medical care. Sarah set about correcting those problems from the moment she took over as superintendent. Things weren't perfect but she surely had begun the process of turning it all around by putting her shoulder to the wheel.

As the bus pulled into the institution's main gate, Annie awoke to the sound of freezing rain pounding the roof of the bus and the aluminum awning covering the walkway that ran parallel to the road used by vehicles entering through the main gate. In a span of four short years, Annie went from being a woman madly in love with a man who swept her off her feet to a woman who would most likely spend the next two decades of her life behind bars for killing the abusive son-of-a-bitch. Her daughter would grow-up believing that her mother had murdered her father. While Sylvia held out hope that they could get a new trial on appeal, Annie had surrendered her hopes of success to the chains of chronic despair.

The newly arriving inmates of MBCCW were greeted by Sergeant Barbara Annis. Sergeant Annis was a portly little woman with a smile that could soothe the soul but a level of professionalism that remained strong as if it were her first day on the job after completing the Correctional Worker Academy, which trained all of the state's prison staff. Annis stepped onto the bus and began a pretty standard welcome speech, explaining that the women would be taken directly to an orientation.

"You'll receive information about the programming that is available to you in hopes that when, and if, you return to society you'll see the error in your ways and change for the better, for yourselves and your families. You'll be issued information about the rules of this institution. Each of you will be given an opportunity to meet with medical and mental health staff to address any important concerns you may have. Any questions? Hearing none, welcome to Mount Baker Corrections Center for Women," ended Sergeant Annis before exiting the crowded bus of female inmates.

CHAPTER 9

After sitting through a 1 ½ hour orientation and being classified as a Medium Custody inmate, Annie was finally taken to her living unit for a cell assignment. While CO Rachel Soren perused the computer system to see if there were any special housing needs for Annie, a female inmate approached her.

"Hey stranger! It's been awhile since I last seen you." Annie immediately recognized her Thurston County Jail cellmate Sibyl Enoch. Both women hugged as if they hadn't seen each other in twenty years. "So I take it your trial didn't go as planned?" Sibyl groaned.

Annie responded, "No, I thought that I had a chance to..."

Sibyl cut Annie off, "You should be careful what you say in front of other inmates because some of these bitches will try to use it against you. So it looks like you're about to be assigned to a cell. Hey CO Soren, why not cell Annie with me? My previous cellmate has been sent to the hole and probably won't be coming back, so I've got a vacancy. Annie and I got along great at the county jail."

CO Soren continued checking the computer system. "Well it appears there's no reason I can't let you two cell together. Are you okay with that Annie?"

"Yes, it's always good to have someone you know to show you around," said Annie.

"Sibyl, you okay with showing Annie to the cell?" asked CO Soren.

"Sure!"

"The rest of your property will be brought to you as soon as it is cleared," added CO Soren. As soon as Sibyl and Annie walked away from her, CO Soren got onto the telephone and started talking to someone while looking at an unsuspecting Annie.

CHAPTER 10

After they had settled in the cell, Annie asked Sibyl a bunch of questions about the prison. Questions like when mail comes in and how often so that she may get some new pictures from her mother of her daughter and correspond with her attorneys as they appealed her conviction. Other questions related to the quality of the food and how to pass the time without going crazy. You know; the things that the orientation doesn't truthfully address. But Sibyl quickly turned the conversation to more important matters. She began speaking in a low and soft voice to Annie. "I've heard that there's some shady goings on here. I've not been able to get anyone to say exactly what but many of the gals here seem to be afraid to tell me. What I've seen with my own eyes is that many of the gals are intimidated by some of the officers."

"Anyone in particular?" asked Annie.

"If I had to guess it seems to be..." Just as Sibyl was about to tell Annie, CO Soren came to the cell and she was accompanied by Sergeant Roy Soren, her husband, who had a face that he often scrunched up giving him the appearance of a man trying very hard to have a bowel movement. Maybe it was the years of heavy smoking and drinking he did before he cleaned up his act. In fact, he could take very little credit for it. Rachel Soren had done most of the heavy lifting. She stood by Roy when she could have easily left him and let him lose his job and his life to alcohol. Rachel got him into a clinic in Mexico that used Ibogaine on chemically dependent addicts. This drug is somewhat of a miracle drug in treating addiction. While it has hallucinogenic side-effects, it's non-addictive and leaves its users free from their prior addiction.

Since getting clean five years ago, Roy and Rachel began experimenting in their sex lives as a way to live life to the fullest. Now they didn't have an open marriage but they did invite other men and women into their marital bed. This was somewhat apparent in their interactions with other people because of the vibe they projected in their contact with others who they found attractive.

CO Soren said, "how y'all adjusting."

Sibyl responded, "Just fine."

Sergeant Soren's eyes lingered on Annie as she sat on her bunk. Annie was not your average female inmate. At about 5' 8" with auburn hair that fell just between her shoulder blades, she had a natural beauty. Throughout much of her life she didn't have the necessity to wear make-up because of it. Roy saw this just as Billy and many other men had. Staring at Annie, Roy said, "What's your name?"

"Annie. Annie Lone," she said uncomfortably because of the tone in his voice.

"Well Annie, welcome to Mount Baker. If you need anything, CO Soren or I can assist you in getting it. Don't hesitate to ask because we'll do anything you want," Sergeant Soren said in an overly smooth and creepy manner.

"O---kay," Annie responded nervously.

CO Soren and Sergeant Soren looked at one another with a turned-on smile on their faces. As they walked away from the cell, their smiles grew wider as if they had discovered some long buried secret.

CHAPTER 11

Annie arrived for the first day of her work assignment in the kitchen. She was immediately sent to work in the scullery. Washing dishes in a place where food is cooked for over a thousand people was hard work, she learned. Not simply because of the quantity of things that needed to be washed but because of the heat from the steam generated in washing the dishes. Beyond washing the dishes there was a great amount of cleaning that was required as well. Floors were mopped several times a day and countertops were sprayed with an antibacterial agent and cleaned all day to meet tough state Department of Health regulations.

At the end of her first day, Annie was exhausted. She had never worked in a service-industry position like this before in her life. Her clothes were soaked with sweat, steam, and a mixture of food and water from spraying the dishes. All she could think about was taking a shower. Getting through this tough day presented her a challenge but she had made it. She made it because she had to fight. She had to fight her way through this experience. Yes she had been convicted but she had a viable appeal. She had Julia and her mother waiting for her on the outside. Before going back to her unit, Annie went looking for her friend Sibyl who worked with the Cooks in the food preparation area.

Annie was told by another inmate who was cutting up some carrots that Sibyl had gone to get something out of the walk-in freezer before her shift ended but she didn't know which one. Annie knew that there were several walk-ins but had no idea which one. Annie reached the walk-in with the meat products in it. She saw a blue hat hanging on the handle of the door. Annie quizzically looked at the hat and then removed it before opening the door. To her surprise she observed a man in a blue uniform with his pants down to his ankles. She couldn't see his face but she knew that the uniform he wore was the uniform worn by the prisons COs. What Annie also observed was that the uniformed man was thrusting his hips forward at a person bent over a stack of boxes in the back of the walk-in. The person appeared to be a woman based on the sounds that she was making whose state-issued inmate pants were down to her ankles as well. The CO continued thrusting behind the female inmate.

There were no sounds of pleasure emanating from the bent over female inmate. Instead, the woman sounded like a wounded animal. She cried out as if she were in excruciating pain. As the woman's anguished sounds of suffering flowed from her mouth, the CO seemed to pick up his pace as he continued to thrust harder and harder into the woman as if he were more aroused by it. Annie was bewildered by what she saw and simply watched in horror with her mouth wide open.

Annie remembered what she had learned in the new inmates' orientation. It was illegal for a state corrections employee to engage in sexual acts with inmates. Annie didn't know what to do. Should she go get someone? Should she yell at the man to stop? What would happen to her if she said anything? She knew that she had to do something because, based on the sounds, the woman was being violated in the worse possible way.

Rape is one of those unforgivable crimes. All of the pain, shame, and fear that Annie had suffered when she had been attacked by Billy over and over again came rushing back to her. She nearly withdrew to the safe place in her mind where she frequently turned during the latter years of her marriage as Billy raped her time and again. But the bravery she had developed to finally stand up to Billy flooded back into her giving her spirit the boost it needed to do what was right and necessary.

Without thinking it entirely through Annie yelled, "Stop!" In a flash, the CO quickly turned around and saw Annie looking at him with a mortified look on her face. The female inmate being raped turned to look at her savior.

"Annie is that you," said the still crying female inmate.

While grabbing for his pants, the unknown CO yelled at Annie saying, "You're out of bounds inmate. I...I'm going to infract you. What the fuck are you doing in here?"

Annie immediately recognized Sibyl. Sibyl looked at Annie with tears in her eyes.

Annie retorted, "What are you doing to my friend? Sibyl, are you alright?"

"Get the fuck out of here inmate," yelled the unknown CO as he pulled up his underwear. Annie saw that his penis was covered in blood and what appeared to be fecal matter.

"Annie..." Sibyl started before being cutoff by the CO as Annie attempted to move toward Sibyl.

However, the CO yelled, "Stay where you are inmate."

"I just want to help my friend," said Annie.

"You heard what I said."

"Just let us leave," responded Annie.

"How about you get the hell out of here." Annie stood there looking at Sibyl. "I mean it. Get out of here," said the CO as he finished zipping up his pants.

At first hesitant, Annie reluctantly left when Sibyl tearfully nodded to her that it was okay. Annie nervously stood outside the door waiting to see her friend emerge from the walk-in. Annie wondered what the CO was doing to Sibyl and hoped he had stopped hurting her. She felt the need to go back in but worried about what he would do to her. Nearly five minutes passed before the partially dressed CO opened the door to the walk-in cooler.

"Get in here," ordered the CO.

"No!" Annie replied not knowing what he had in store for her.

Without making a scene and in a quiet voice while leaning directly toward her, he threatened, "You better keep your fucking mouth shut or you may not be able to open it ever again."

With that said, he stalked off as if nothing had happened buttoning the remainder of his shirt. Annie was so afraid that she hadn't paid attention to the name on the CO's uniform. Peering around the corner, just out of earshot, was an unknown female inmate who looked upset but Annie didn't notice her as her mind was on Sibyl's wellbeing. She rushed back into the walk-in and found Sibyl despondent lying on the floor. Annie immediately went to her.

"I can't believe that he would do this to me," cried Sibyl. "What did I do to deserve this?"

"Nothing. These guys are just fucking animals. Uncivilized fucking animals who think they can take whatever they want," she replied. As Sibyl continued to sob, Annie just held her in arms in a futile attempt to comfort her. She didn't ask Sibyl any questions about what happened. She knew better not to. She had suffered the same humiliating assault. She knew that at this moment in time Sibyl needed a friend not an inquest. Annie also knew that something had to be done about this rape but it wouldn't be tonight. It took Annie nearly forty-five minutes to get Sibyl back to their cell. Aside from having to deal with her pending appeal, Annie had also discovered that she had an even bigger problem. The problem of staying in one piece in this prison.

CHAPTER 12

Over the next two days Annie kept a close watch on Sibyl who refused to report the fact that she had been raped despite all of Annie's protestations. What she had witnessed bewildered her. These people, the COs, were supposed to protect the inmates. Instead, here was a CO violently raping her friend. She always knew and understood that there were uncaring, even cruel, people in life but this was too much. This was a prison. This was one of the institutions that society expected would confine and punish lawbreakers as well as reform them before returning them to society. How would raping the inmates serve that purpose?

Annie's mental images of prison life were similar to those of most Americans. She believed that inmates sat around daily enjoying their incarcerated life of three hots and a cot along with the supposed excellent medical care they received while housed in these institutions. As Annie began to quickly learn, public perception was quite different from the reality of incarceration. In fact, Annie got a firsthand view of the fallacy of this belief.

Sibyl told Annie when she first arrived about the rumors she had heard about. Now she knew what the rumors were related to; the COs engaging in sexual relations, forced and coerced, with female inmates. Sibyl hadn't observed it first hand but she eventually became a victim of it. Annie racked her brain trying to figure out what to do to help the despondent Sibyl. Eventually she began mentally replaying the prison rape informational session they had during inmate orientation hoping to find something that she could do to help Sibyl.

What stood out in her mind was that much of the focus was on inmate-on-inmate rape as well as inmate manipulation of prison staff with very little attention to prison staff that target inmates. While certainly Mount Baker Corrections Center for Women has the problem of inmate-on-inmate rape like most prisons, the crimes discovered by Annie and perpetrated against Sibyl, however, were staff-on-inmate rape. Annie tended to Sibyl while simultaneously reviewing the prison rape materials she received during the orientation. The booklet discussed the primary causes of sexual misconduct between prison inmates and prison staff. She quickly read the section titled _Inmate Manipulation_.

According to the booklet, the inmates who manipulate prison staff look for prison staff members that are having marital/relationship problems, those who become overly familiar with the inmates, or those who are simply lonely in their personal lives. Often times, the inmates expect to gain some type of advantage from having the sexual relationship with the prison staff member like receiving contraband items such as cigarettes, illicit drugs, and disallowed movies. For this reason, correctional training teaches staff members not to discuss personal matters in the presence of inmates and to be aware that inmates will try to manipulate you into doing something you should not.

The goal was to keep the prison staff professional with inmates at all time and avoid becoming personally involved with inmates. Inmates were warned that if they are caught trying to manipulate staff they would be subject to an infraction for violating prison rules. Staff were also warned that they may be subject to discipline for engaging in a sexual relationship with inmates. After reviewing this section Annie was disappointed because it said nothing about Sibyl's particular situation.

What was whispered about and what Annie witnessed at MBCCW was distinct. Prison staff members coerced or forced female inmates to engage in sexual acts. While in the prison law library, Annie came across a law review article that shed some light on the subject of prison rape. She found that forced sexual acts were covered by most states' Rape laws. But the coerced and/or consensual sexual acts were generally not covered by existing Rape laws. As a result, many states enacted laws banning correctional staff members from engaging in sexual acts with inmates in much the same way that state law protects minors below a certain age with statutory rape laws after several publicly embarrassing examples of staff-on-inmate sex came to light.

This happened in Washington State in 1999 when the legislature adopted WASH. REV. CODE §§ 9A.44.160 and 9A.44.170 (Custodial Sexual Misconduct in the first degree and in the second degree respectively) to prohibit staff members and contractors from engaging in sexual intercourse and sexual contact with inmates respectively. The new law stripped inmates of the ability to consent to such acts on the grounds that they were wards of the state when they were incarcerated and should be protected from staff members' sexual advances.

Despite these legislative reforms in Washington, here Sibyl and Annie were right in the middle of a tumult of sexual abuse and violence. Annie had so many things on her mind. How could something like this go unnoticed and unreported? How long had this prison been this way? She wanted to find some answers but right now her priority was her friend so Annie hurried back to her cell to check on Sibyl.

Sibyl slept for extended periods of time. She barely touched any food. She took several days off work by complaining of headaches in sick call. Sibyl's experience severely changed the normally open and talkative woman into a person who became withdrawn and a shell of herself.

"Sibyl! It's time for us to go to lunch. Are you ready?" asked Annie.

"Yeah let's go," Sibyl replied. As the two

women exited their cell, Sibyl immediately froze and stared at the uniformed man standing near the control booth. Annie, not realizing what had happened, tried to get her to snap out of it. Noticing the two female inmates, the uniformed man approached them. Annie looked up and saw him approaching. She immediately recognized him from the walk-in. This man was the rapist who had forced himself on Sibyl. Annie's heart began to pound uncontrollably. What was this son-of-a-bitch doing here? Had he come to retaliate against them?

"Hello ladies. I'm Captain Doyle Draper and...," said the uniformed man acting as if he didn't know the women and looking at a jittery Sibyl.

Annie responded, "You stay the hell away from me and my friend."

"You show me some respect in my prison," yelled Captain Draper. "If you don't you'll end up in Segregation. I'm only here to help your friend. You got that?"

Annie didn't respond.

"Did you hear me?" Captain Draper retorted.

"Yes sir!" Annie acquiesced to his assertion of authority.

"Good," responded Captain Draper before walking off. She realized immediately that she was in no position to challenge him. As she contemplated her next move, she saw Captain Draper talking to another uniformed man on their unit who pointed to her and Sibyl. Annie recognized him as Lieutenant Lance Atron who she had first seen at her prison orientation. Seeing both of these high-ranking correctional officials together made Annie completely aware of the predicament she faced within the prison. How would she be able to seek help for Sibyl under these circumstances? After thinking for a few minutes, Annie decided there was a much more effective way to deal with this problem.

Upon returning to their cell after lunch, Sibyl laid down to take a nap. Annie began writing a letter to Sylvia about what she witnessed happen to Sibyl. When Annie started writing, her thoughts just poured out of her. She asked Sylvia for help in dealing with Captain Draper and getting help for Sibyl after the attack because she seemed depressed. She expressed her intentions of filing a formal grievance about what she had seen happen to Sibyl despite her fear of retaliation by Captain Draper but wanted Sylvia's input first.

As Annie continued writing the letter, she also explained that she had learned that there were rumors of an organized and ongoing systemic problem of staff members having sexual relationships with inmates. This information came from other inmates during lunch mainline including the fact that Captain Draper and many other COs had been engaging in sexual relations with female inmates for years. Annie made clear that none of the women were willing to go on the record out of fear; fear that they would be snitched out by inmates who were willing participants in these sexual trysts. After finishing up the letter, Annie hurriedly put her stuff away because she had a meeting, arranged through other inmates, with a fellow inmate who was willing to give more detail about what had happened at MBCCW over the years.

The inmate, named Carol Plat, agreed to meet Annie in the shower. Annie quickly gathered her towel and toiletries and headed to the shower area. Carol chose the shower area for its relative privacy from prying ears. If you're there at the right time there are very few inmates showering. Additionally, turning on a shower will make it harder for anyone to listen to what you're saying. Even more importantly, the COs were not generally in there long as they simply passed through doing security checks.

Once two shower heads were turned on, Carol told Annie her story in detail. Carol had been in prison for twenty-two years after being convicted for killing her husband using poison for insurance money and then setting fire to the family home to make it look like an accident. When she arrived at the prison, she was a twenty-six year old redhead that plucked and preened in front of mirrors for hours making herself perfect to please men and to manipulate them. Carol continued to wear heavy amounts of make-up and got all dolled-up after she arrived at MBCCW. So of course she attracted the attention of the staff members who had been engaging in these sexual relationships with inmates. She got whatever she wanted too.

Staff members allowed her to go out of bounds on a regular basis to make phone calls to friends and family members. In prison, allowing an inmate to go out of bounds was a huge security risk because it meant that an inmate had access to secure areas of the prison and the opportunity to engage in mischief or worse. These areas were generally secure and off-limits to inmates because they either presented an opportunity for an inmate to escape, attack a prison staff member, or get access to prison weapons. Regardless of the reasoning, Carol had the run of the place so long as she was willing to give herself to the COs who wanted her. They also provided her with prohibited items including the latest music, movies to watch, wine to drink, and weed to smoke. She even convinced a CO to take her out of the institution to catch a movie she heard about from one of her family members.

Now at the age of forty-eight, she had abandoned that façade for a make-up-less appearance that showed the age lines and damage done by years of covering her face in heavy make-up. With her aging and the turnover in prison personnel over the years, fewer and fewer of the COs wanted to be with her anyway but she was okay with it. She had started becoming a different person; different from the young, horny woman who wanted the attention of the men around her. This was largely due to her realization that while she thought she was exploiting the male staff members they were actually exploiting her by treating her like an object; a mere piece of meat that could be passed around from man-to-man without any consideration of her feelings.

Yes, she had been a willing participant but she was fucked up. Fucked up because, as a young woman, she didn't respect herself enough to see that she had a brain; that she was not just tits-and-ass. Yeah, she looked good when she put effort into it but that was not the entire substance of who she was. The prison staff should have pointed that out to her. That is what prison is supposed to be about; identifying the mistakes that a person made to land them in prison in the first place and helping them learn how to avoid those mistakes in the future. That, by in large, is the reason society changed the position title from Prison Guard to Correctional Officer.

Part of redirecting inmates included correcting inappropriate behavior and teaching the inmates self-respect in conjunction with a wide array of programs. The programs that prisons offer are designed to address chemical dependency issues, mental health problems, self-esteem deficiencies, the lack of job skills and education; a litany of things that could be core reasons for a person getting off track in life. The point is that prison staff should have encouraged her to get counseling to help her understand why she presented herself to men as a mere sex object. Instead, they took advantage of this vulnerable person.

"So this place is really fucked up?" whispered Annie.

"Well, of course it is," replied Carol. "Many of these girls in here are like I used to be. They think they can have a relationship with these COs."

"I haven't met one of them yet that does," added Annie.

"Yes you have. I heard about your run-in with Hannah Jane. She's Draper's girl. Anyway that's one type of girl we have here at Mount Baker. These girls get to have MP3 players, cell phones, weed, and all sorts of other shit. So long as they put out they get what they want."

"Sounds a lot like prostitution to me?" queried Annie.

"That's not far from the truth. The other type of girl here at Mount Baker is the one who needs to be convinced. These girls don't want to have sex with the COs. Even if they don't want to fuck, the COs will, either by manipulation or force, fuck these girls too. So either way it is a win-win for the COs who do this."

"Not all of the COs are in on it?"

"That's right. But enough of them are that it makes it dangerous to know who to trust and where to turn."

"Damn! My friend Sibyl was forcibly raped by Captain Draper."

"I'm sorry to hear that but there was a girl here named Jessica. I believe it was Jessica Wick. She had some mental problems. She told everybody that she had been sent up on an Arson conviction, which was hard to believe because she was so young and meek looking. I tell you it was hard to see her that way. I thought if anything she was here for forgery or identity theft or some minor bullshit like that. But anyway, I guess Captain Draper came onto her and she didn't immediately drop her drawers for him."

"What did he do to her?" asked Annie.

"Captain Draper, Lieutenant Atron and two COs brutally raped Jessica for over three hours. Three fucking hours! All to *teach* her a lesson. Then she killed herself," said Carol.

"Did anyone report this?"

"Of course not! And even if they did there would be no evidence of it."

"Not even DNA or vaginal tearing?" inquired Annie.

"Nope. They used rubbers. They even doctored up an incident report of Jessica being raped by an inmate who had escaped from the prison's mental health unit."

"This is like a damned nightmare," said Annie. "When did this place get this way?"

"After all my years here I still don't know when this all started," exclaimed Carol.

"Somebody's got to put a stop to it. We're not put here to amuse and satisfy their sick and twisted desires," said Annie.

"Annie, whatever you do? Be careful. These SOBs have eyes and ears everywhere. People you wouldn't even suspect."

"Thanks for the advice."

Annie remained in the shower for another five minutes after Carol left. She wondered whether her letter to Sylvia would do any good. Annie lingered on the issue of whether to file a formal grievance with the prison administration since Captain Draper headed the uniformed staff members of the prison. She turned off the shower and started drying herself off. After wrapping her hair in a towel, she got dressed quickly to get back to her cell to check on Sibyl. As she exited the shower area, the inmate who appeared outside the walk-in showed up.

"I saw you talking to Captain Draper. You know he and I have something special," said the unknown female inmate.

"Okay?" replied Annie. "So you're Hannah Jane?"

"Yes," she responded. "I guess you don't know what everyone else here knows, which is to stay away from Captain Draper. He's mine. When I get released, we're going to get married." Hannah Jane, a woman in her mid-forties still bearing some of her youthful good looks despite the relatively hard life she had led that put a few wrinkles in strategic places on her face, seethed anger in her every word to Annie.

"I have no interest in Captain Draper. I just want to do my time," Annie said.

"I saw you talking to Draper...seemed to me you were all over him. I just want you to be on notice that he's mine," responded Hannah.

"Like I said, I have no interest in the creep," retorted Annie.

"You know...that's bullshit. Little bitches like yourself come in here and pretend you're not interested in him but as soon as I turn my back you're spreading your stinking legs in front of him trying to get his attention."

"Rest assured that I won't be spreading anything in front of him," Annie quipped.

Annie tried to walk around her but Hannah Jane blocked her. Annie thought for sure that she was about to have her first prison fight. Noticing a CO coming toward them, she slinked off but not before giving Annie a threatening look.

"Everything alright here?" asked the CO.

"Yeah. Yeah. There's no problem," answered Annie.

"Okay. Well, when I saw Hannah Jane step in front of you I thought she was about to hit you. She's a bit of a fighter so when I see her I try to step in and deescalate a situation before an altercation occurs."

"Nope, everything's okay."

As the CO walked off, Annie immediately remembered Carol's statement about some inmates being willing participants. But this seemed different. This woman, Hannah Jane, had planned a future with Captain Draper after her release from this prison. Walking back to her cell, Annie's mind remained fixed on what Hannah Jane had told her about Captain Draper. Had it been a lie? Surely it must have been. Would he marry her and be with her after she was released from prison? It sure didn't sound believable. How could a man who professes love for one woman turn around and rape another woman? She really didn't believe what Hannah Jane had told her. Especially in light of the fact that he brutally raped Jessica and Sibyl; who knew how many other inmates he had been involved with both consensually and forcibly.

Either way, did Hannah Jane not know about

these things or was he convincingly lying to her about what was happening? You know the standard lie some men tell, "I slipped and accidentally fell cock first into that other woman who had her legs spread in front of me." Many women believe this story as told by their significant other in its many variations. Annie certainly believed that Hannah Jane was one of those women because she was completely in blame-the-other-woman mode when they met. Annie returned to the cell and immediately woke Sibyl to tell her what she had learned from Carol as well as about Hannah Jane's threat.

"Watch out for her. She has a reputation for violence and sounds like she wants to hurt you. When I first got here my first cellmate told me that she had bitten another woman's ear off in a fight," said Sibyl.

"Why the hell is she walking around here like she owns the place?" asked Annie.

"Because she *is* Captain Draper's girl...that's why," Sibyl said. "Please Annie; you have to promise that you'll steer clear of that woman."

"Okay I'll do my best but as I said she actually approached me," said Annie.

"Let's just hope we can serve the rest of our time without anymore bullshit happening," Sibyl said as she lay back down on her bed.

CHAPTER 13

Captain Draper sat in the chair in front of Associate Superintendent Jennifer Welch's desk. Jennifer had been with the state corrections system for nearly twenty years. She and Draper had dated for a brief time before he married his current wife. Even after his marriage, he and Jennifer continued seeing each other. Any man would have a hard time turning down the 5'4" 105 pound brunette. What she lacked in bust-size, she more than made up for in athleticism and enthusiasm in the bedroom.

Jennifer had started life on the straight and narrow. She had graduated from Seattle State University with a B.S. in Biology but had a long burning urge to join law enforcement. This urge was primarily developed in her adolescence when she saw weaker children being bullied and beaten in her rough Los Angeles neighborhood. In the beginning, all she wanted to do was help people. At some point, her career plan to make other people's lives better went off the rails. Jennifer didn't seem to know exactly when and where she got off track. All she knew was she couldn't let it come out that she knew about the sexual abuse and rape taking place at MBCCW. She shutoff her computer and sat back in her chair with a worried look on her face.

"I hope you guys are being careful," Jennifer declared.

"We are," smirked Captain Draper.

"Seriously this new bitch will bring us all down if she finds out that there are staff members fucking around with the offenders."

"She won't. You know most superintendents don't know half of the shit that goes on in their prisons. She'll know even less."

"Don't be arrogant about it. We know her reputation."

"Yes we do. But we have a good system here Jennifer."

"Well, I've been debating about shutting the whole thing down."

Draper stood up, "You can't."

"Sit down. I've only been thinking about it. I just don't want the lot of us led out of here in damned handcuffs."

"We've got everything under control."

"The minute something happens that could jeopardize our freedom we've got to get out in front of it and bury any trace that this was ever going on."

"Agreed. We've been doing this here for the past thirty-five years. I think we know how to handle these inmate bitches."

"Alright then. But you need to know that I'm not taking the fall for anybody Draper. Not even you."

"You won't have to."

As Draper exited the office, he continued to smirk. Jennifer Welch was more concerned. She knew that Superintendent Sarah Loons was a pit bull. Once she got a hold of something, she wouldn't let it go. Jennifer remembered how much attention the headlines garnered when Sarah arrived at MBCCW a short while ago. She understood that Sarah would have wide discretion in the management of the institution and might well uncover the vile sex ring started nearly four decades earlier by her father and his colleagues.

CHAPTER 14

After a couple of days of missing work in the kitchen, Sibyl returned to her normal duties with Annie. The two women went to their separate work areas after giving each other a huge hug.

"If you need me, come and get me or send someone for me," whispered Annie.

"I'll be okay," replied Sibyl as she walked down the hallway. Annie started toward the scullery still a bit worried about Sibyl going back to work so soon.

Annie immediately started getting her stuff setup when she reached the scullery. During meal times this place was extremely busy as the dishes piled up quickly. So in an effort to stay ahead of the game Annie gathered the cleaning supplies she needed for the day. After having collected a set of rubber gloves, sponges, and other items, Annie asked the CO in charge of the scullery for permission to retrieve the mop and bucket she needed because the CO would have to unlock the door to the area where they were stored along with the cleaning agents Annie used that also had to be dispensed by the CO. Too lazy to open the door, the CO handed Annie the key.

Annie reached the storage closet and opened the door using the key given to her by the CO. In the closet, Annie heard some faint sounds. It was as if a person was huffing and puffing. She stood still and started listening intently. It sounded like someone was working out in a gym lifting weights. After moving around the small storage closet trying to locate where the sound was coming from, she gave up and grabbed the mop and bucket. Closing the door behind her, Annie saw light coming from an adjacent room. She slowly crept down the corridor toward the room. Annie kneeled by the door and looked under it. She saw Sergeant Soren and CO Soren engaged in sexual relations with another person. Sergeant Soren was standing behind the other woman with his pants down at his ankles thrusting into her. CO Soren was kissing the woman and fondling her breasts.

The scene shocked Annie. So much so that she lost her balance and bumped the door. Sergeant Soren immediately stopped and pulled up his pants. Annie jumped up from the door and started quietly trying to walk out of the area but the door hastily opened and Sergeant Soren came out.

"Hey Annie! Come here," demanded Sergeant Soren.

Annie stopped walking and slowly turned toward Sergeant Soren.

"I said come here inmate," Sergeant Soren said again. "Let's talk."

Sergeant Soren pointed inside the room. Annie initially hesitated. Then she entered the room. Inside she saw CO Soren and the woman, who Annie now recognized as another inmate from her unit, in various stages of undress but putting their clothes on.

"Hey guys you don't have to get dressed. Just hold up," said Sergeant Soren. Looking at Annie, he said, "So you obviously are curious about what we're doing here."

"No...No I'm not. I'm just here for the mop and bucket for the scullery," replied Annie.

"There's no need to be ashamed," said CO Soren. "When I discovered that I was bisexual, Roy was completely accommodating of my needs. If you want to join us, I'm definitely okay with it."

"No thanks. I just want to get back to the scullery."

"Well, you know Rachel and I noticed you when you first got here. We both think you're so beautiful. We can make your life here so much easier if you ever want to take Rachel up on her offer to join us," added Sergeant Soren.

"No, this isn't for me. I like men...I mean I just want to serve my time," said Annie nervously.

"That's too bad. I would make you cum so hard your head would spin," taunted CO Soren.

"It's true. She has a magical technique. Since

your deciding not to join us we would prefer it if you would keep this quiet. Anyway, too bad it's your loss," said Sergeant Soren.

Annie, still a little nervous but relieved, responded, "Your secret is safe with me."

Sergeant Soren opened the door for Annie to leave. He looked at Annie from head-to-toe with a longing of a hungry man who hadn't eaten in days. It scared Annie a little.

"Alright Annie, you can go now. We'll see you around," said Sergeant Soren. With that said, Annie slinked out of the room and back to the scullery with a sense of relief.

CHAPTER 15

When Annie's shift in the kitchen ended she returned to her cell for a nap after having taken a shower in preparation for an important day. This was a day she had looked forward to since her arrival at MBCCW. At about 1 p.m., Annie was anticipating a call out to the visit room as her mother had previously written her informing her that she and Julia would come to see her. Annie smiled with excitement at the chance to see Julia. She missed her mother too but Julia was at the center of Annie's thoughts. She loved that baby girl with every fiber of her being. As the clock ticked past 1 p.m. and closer to 2 p.m., Annie grew worried, frustrated, and more than a little upset. Daryn still hadn't arrived with Julia.

"My mom was supposed to come today with Julia. I haven't heard a thing. Something must be wrong," sighed Annie.

"Not to sound paranoid, Annie, I doubt you'll see another visitor or receive another letter from anyone," Sibyl said.

"What do you mean?" inquired Annie.

"Well, the girl who committed suicide had been completely isolated. Rumor has it, she hadn't had any communication with the outside world her last six weeks at this prison," explained Sibyl.

"You mean to tell me that my mother actually showed up and was turned away?" asked Annie.

"That's probably the case," replied Sibyl.

Realizing the bind that she was in, Annie called for the Unit Sergeant, Roy Soren.

"What do you need beautiful?" replied Sergeant Soren.

"Sergeant Soren, I need to send a kite to the Superintendent, Associate Superintendent, or anyone who'll listen."

"What's the problem?" asked Sergeant Soren.

"I just want a kite," responded Annie.

"Well let me get you one," he said hesitantly.

Returning with the inmate kite in hand, Sergeant Soren handed it to Annie. She went to the desk in her cell and began filling it out. Inmates use kites in prisons to informally raise complaints about prison conditions, staff, or other issues. It was Annie's first time using the kite system in the prison. Sibyl stood by with a pained look on her face. She wanted to yell at Annie to stop before she ended up being a rape victim at the hands of the prison staff but she was paralyzed by fear. She feared being targeted again herself.

Sergeant Soren returned to his post and immediately got on his radio. Sibyl watched as Sergeant Soren's wife, CO Rachel Soren, arrived and the two talked briefly before CO Soren left the unit quickly. When she finished writing the kite, Annie called for Sergeant Soren and handed it to him.

CHAPTER 16

Annie couldn't sleep well that night, her mind raced as she thought of all the reasons why her mother hadn't shown up. She obsessively focused on not getting to see her baby, Julia, that day as planned. She wanted so much to hug and kiss her baby girl. It had been so long.

Many women in prison have limited or no bond at all with their children because most of them are drug addicted criminals who abandoned their children with relatives or to the custody of the state in favor of running the streets in search of fun in the form of sex, alcohol, and drugs.

This was not Annie Lone. Annie had a strong bond with Julia, which made it all the more difficult for her to be locked up in prison and unable to be with her. She knew her mother would do a good job looking after Julia but Annie's own maternal instincts told her that she had to be with Julia, had to take care of her, and, even more, had to let her know how much she loved her every single day. Being in this prison made it extremely hard for Annie to live up to her motherly responsibility, which was all she could think about. It simply tore her up inside.

Just after midnight, an unknown male CO came to Annie's cell to get her telling her that she had an emergency phone call. Trying to shake off the drowsiness as she exited her cell to follow the CO, Annie rubbed the sleep out of her eyes. As she traversed the prison's corridors accompanied by the CO, Annie wondered what the emergency was. Maybe her mother was ill and had to put Julia in someone else's care. God forbid her dear daughter could be ill. Annie's mind wandered over the array of possible emergencies.

As she arrived at her prison counselor's office, Annie's nervousness grew exponentially at the possible emergency. The CO guided her past the counselor's door and toward Captain Draper's Office. The CO knocked on the counselor's closed door. As the door swung open, Annie saw Captain Draper standing inside opening it. Annie reflexively took a step backward as if she were readying herself to flee the scene of something horrific bumping into the CO who had accompanied her. A panic washed over her. She knew that he would certainly try to rape her in the same way he had attacked Sibyl. Annie gathered her thoughts and prepared herself for the biggest fight of her life. She was not going to let this happen.

"Come in Annie," said Captain Draper.

"What's the emergency?" asked Annie.

"We'll talk about that and more. Come on in," said the now insistent Captain.

As Annie slowly advanced into the office, she scanned the small room in an effort to spot a route of escape or possible weapons she could use when Captain Draper attempted to force himself on her. To no avail, Annie didn't see anything that would assist her in fending off a potential attack or a way to make a quick exit other than the door she used to enter the 5' by 7' room that must have been an equipment storage closet before its conversion into a makeshift office.

After closing the door, Captain Draper posted up in front of the only exit and began by saying, "There comes a time when one has to find out if one is a team player or an individual. Team players tend to cooperate with the mission. They tend to unite for a common cause. After reading this letter you wrote to this Sylvia Gray, it's become abundantly clear that you're not on our team. I'll give you one last chance to make this mistake of yours right. First, I need you to take off your clothes and get down on your knees."

Realizing the predicament she was in Annie said, "I know my rights! And what you and the other poor excuses for prison guards are doing here is illegal as hell."

"Hey, that's COs."

"What?"

"Corrections and Custody Officers. COs not prison guards."

"Okay, COs," Annie relented. "Either way, I'm not taking off..."

"And I see I haven't been able to get through to you."

With those words, Captain Draper opened the door that he stood in front of and three unknown COs rushed in and grabbed Annie. They began shouting that she had assaulted a prison staff member and subdued her using arm bars before placing her in cuffs. One officer yelled that assault on a prison staff member was a serious infraction that could result in severe prison discipline.

In an absolute state of shock, Annie surrendered to their use of force. She realized that the surprise sprung upon her in the middle of night had been well planned and thought out. Annie's despair over not seeing Julia and her mother grew as the COs dragged her down the corridors of the prison to the Segregation Unit.

CHAPTER 17

Daryn unlocked the door and pressed the button to close the garage door. The drive from Whatcom County back to her Olympia home had been long and grueling. She put Julia on the floor and she toddled off toward a toy she saw laying nearby in the kitchen. Daryn, now fifty-nine years old, hadn't taken care of a child in decades but it was sort of like a bicycle. Once you get back on it, it comes right back to you. That fact didn't abate the anxiety she felt. Nevertheless she knew that Annie needed her, which helped squelch the nervousness.

Daryn walked into the kitchen and started looking around for ideas for dinner. She noticed the message light on the telephone glowing bright red. The message was from Annie's lawyer, Sylvia.

"Hi Mrs. Mallory. I'm calling because I've not heard from Annie for a while. I sent her several letters but received no responses from her. Just wondering if you've heard from her and know if she's okay. Anyway give me a call when you get a chance at (206) 555-1234. I hope to hear from you soon."

Daryn hung up the phone and pondered how completely out of character it was for Annie not to stay in contact with Sylvia. This coupled with the fact that Annie was in Segregation for disciplinary matters on the very day she knew that Daryn was bringing Julia for a visit seemed too strange to be real. She knew how much Annie wanted to appeal her conviction. Even more, she knew how much her daughter suffered being separated from Julia.

Daryn's concern turned to sadness at the thought that maybe prison was getting the best of Annie. Maybe she had given up on getting out. Maybe the place was beating her down; beating her down so much so that she couldn't cope with the reality of incarceration. Daryn decided that she needed to help her daughter. She looked at the clock and realized that it was 5:30. There would be no one in Sylvia's law office this late for her to talk to; at least at the front desk, where the phones are answered. In the morning, she would pay Sylvia a visit. Right now she needed to give all of her attention to Julia. Daryn scooped the toddler up off the floor and started hugging her. As little Julia thrashed about laughing frantically, Daryn's mind was freed from the worry of Annie for just a few moments.

"It's good you got here early," said the secretary. "Follow me this way."

"Thank you," Daryn replied. The secretary led Daryn down a hallway to a large office in the corner of the building.

"Come on in Ms. Mallory," said Sylvia as she stood to shake hands with Daryn. "Please close the door behind you, Imogene."

"You got it," Imogene responded.

"So you got my message. I haven't heard anything from Annie in a while and I've sent her several letters. Have you heard anything?" asked Sylvia.

"No I haven't. I drove up to the prison to see her yesterday with Julia but they told me that she was in Segregation for a disciplinary matter," said Daryn.

"Did they say what the disciplinary matter was about?" inquired Sylvia.

"No. No they didn't."

"Did they say how long she had been in Segregation?"

"Nope."

"Well I can look into it. Don't worry Mrs. Mallory. I'll get on it right away."

"Thank you. I'm just so worried about Annie. I started thinking the worst. You know. That she had given up on life. Given up on Julia."

"No way would she do that Ms. Mallory. I talked to her thoroughly and Julia is the center of her life. One thing I know is that that woman loves that little girl and would never abandon her. I'll get my team working on it right away."

"Again, thank you so much."

"It's my job and my pleasure."

Daryn and Sylvia shook hands and Daryn picked up Julia and left the office. Sylvia's smile grew into a concerned look as Daryn departed. From what she had learned about Annie, her lack of communication was out of character. She would have to make a special trip up to MBCCW to visit Annie and check on her personally to make sure she hadn't given up on trying to get out of that place.

CHAPTER 18

After her prison disciplinary hearing for the trumped up serious infraction for assaulting Captain Draper, Annie sat in her Segregation cell for twenty-three hours a day for the next ten days. During that time, she received no mail from Sylvia about her case or from her mother about her daughter Julia. She had only been in prison a few days and here she was in a world of trouble. She wondered about her precious child day and night. She thought about how to effect positive change for herself and the other women at MBCCW. It was quite apparent to her that the isolation was meant to break her. She was never given the required portion sizes for her meals that met the recommended dietary caloric intake for an adult woman, her one hour of yard time was always cut short by fifteen minutes, and none of the prison staff ever talked to her. But she realized what they were doing to her so she focused on her plan.

With all of the channels of communication in

and out of the prison in the control of the prison staff, Annie knew that the chances of communicating with the outside world would be nearly impossible. Thus, Annie had to find another way. Just as she sat in the corner contemplating what she considered to be the only plan available to her, the cell door opened and Sergeant Roy Soren and his wife, CO Rachel Soren, from her unit entered.

"Annie, we have had our eye on you for quit some time," said Rachel, "and we can make your stay here at Mount Baker easier if you're willing to play ball."

"I've already had Captain Draper make advances toward me. I don't need it from you guys," snapped Annie.

In one quick movement, Sergeant Soren grabbed Annie by the neck and pushed her against the wall. "You dumb bitch. Don't you realize how much you could gain here if you just cooperate? We can get you *special* visits with your daughter and mother, any kind of food, and damn near anything else. But you want to throw it all away for pride," he shouted.

"I just want to serve my time and get the hell out of here," retorted Annie as she forcefully moved out of Sergeant Soren's grasp.

Leaning against the cell door, CO Soren responded, "You can serve your time in relative comfort. All that Roy and I want is to spend a little intimate time getting to know you better. I can be the best friend you have here. I can protect you from all of the other custody staff if they know that we have something special between us."

"Well, that's not happening. All that I want is to be left alone," said Annie.

"You're so beautiful Annie. I would give almost anything for…" Annie cut her off by saying, "You're a woman yourself. How could you let these men rape and degrade other women like this? What the hell is wrong with you?"

"Rape and degrade?" asked CO Soren, "No one is being raped here. These women know exactly what they're doing and get what they want out of it."

"How do you explain what happened to the woman who committed suicide? How do you explain what happened to my cellmate Sibyl Enoch?" shouted Annie.

"Raped? That woman who killed herself was mentally ill and always tried to make advances at staff members. As far as I know, Sibyl Enoch and Captain Draper was entirely consensual," responded CO Soren.

"Get the hell out of my cell. Both of you! And leave me alone!" Annie said in an angry voice.

"Be careful what you ask for," a visibly angered Sergeant Soren said. He and his wife walked out of the cell and closed the door.

Annie sat down on her bunk and a tear rolled down her cheek. She released a great big sigh because she was able to resist the advances of the Sorens. The two of them approaching her only cemented in her mind the action that she needed to take in order to protect herself and the other inmates. As she lay down on her bunk that night, she started planning the initial steps to execute her plan to let the world know what was taking place at the prison.

CHAPTER 19

The next time her cell door opened an unknown male CO announced that her stay in Segregation would end. Annie hadn't realized that her time had passed so fast.

"When will I be receiving my mail?" Annie asked the CO.

"If you have any, it should be given to you when you go back to your cell," the CO responded gruffly.

Upon arrival back at her cell, Annie noticed that Sibyl seemed even more withdrawn than the last time she had seen her. Sibyl didn't look up when Annie entered the cell despite the noise of the cell door being closed. Annie slowly approached her so as not to frighten her.

"Sibyl! It's me, your friend, Annie."

"Oh Annie! I am so glad to see you. It's about time they released you from that cage," Sibyl said as she grabbed Annie and tightly hugged her.

"How have things been since I was put in Seg?"

"I think you're in danger Annie," Sibyl said as she began to cry.

"Why are you crying?"

"That inmate who stopped by, what's her name, Hannah Jane, she came by again this time to leave you a message."

"What message?"

Becoming more upset, Sibyl said, "To tell you the truth she was going to hurt you bad for going after Captain Draper. She said she knows that you were with him one night because a friend of hers saw you being taken out of the cell by some of Draper's guys, the same guys who used to come get her out of her cell for her liaisons with Captain Draper."

"Well, she's going to find out that nothing happened between us."

"She said she knows that something happened because Draper doesn't even want to be with her anymore. She said that he hasn't sent for her in a while."

"That has nothing to do with me."

"Annie, I have something else to tell you. After delivering her message, she and two other inmates held me down and took turns performing oral sex on

95

me and making me perform it to them."

"Oh Sibyl!" said Annie as she put her arms around her in an effort to comfort her.

"They're not going to get away with this. There's no way in hell I'm going to let that happen," declared Annie as she was fuming with anger.

CHAPTER 20

The next day, Annie and Sibyl sat on a bench in the corner of the big yard people-watching as the other inmates milled around. Mount Baker, standing tall, loomed large over the prison with its heavily snow-capped peak. It was one of those rare clear winter days in Northwest Washington. While it was clear, it was bitterly cold. The atmosphere on the yard was rather relaxed and sedate until Annie spotted Hannah Jane standing near the softball diamond. Annie leapt to her feet and began to approach Hannah Jane. Sibyl grabbed for Annie's hand but missed it because of the speed with which Annie got up. Annie knew that if she ran toward her the COs on the yard would immediately respond and prevent her from ever making it to Hannah Jane and she definitely wanted her shot at her. Her mind focused entirely on what they had done to Sibyl while she was in Segregation.

As she drew closer to Hannah Jane, her heart

began racing at an uncontrollable pace. Hannah Jane looked over and saw Annie closing in on her and took a fighting stance. Annie didn't hesitate in her gait as she locked her eyes on Hannah Jane. Just before the two collided Hannah Jane said, "It's about time you had the stomach to come and face me you man stealing bitch."

As Annie reached Hannah Jane's location and took a swing at her, two COs, unbeknownst to both women, had spotted their collision course and moved to prevent it from taking place. A male CO took Annie to the ground and a female CO stepped in between them to prevent any cheap shots while simultaneously radioing for assistance. Lying on the ground Annie shouted, "This isn't over. Not by a long shot. You should have stayed away from Sibyl."

"Anytime Soccer Mom. Anytime!" retorted Hannah Jane, "I'll be here waiting for you."

As Annie lay upon the ground being cuffed she realized that there must be a better way to deal with her anger and fear. Attacking Hannah Jane would give her a short term sense of relief for her sorrow about Sibyl's pain but it would do nothing for the overall sense of insecurity she felt being trapped in this institution of *correction* as merely a piece of meat on display and ready for the taking at anytime by the corrupt staff. This incident made her realize the flaw in her original plan. As the COs lifted her off the ground she realized that she had to go back to drawing board.

CHAPTER 21

After returning to her cell from yet another stint in Segregation for her attempted assault on Hannah Jane, Annie had an entirely new outlook. "Hi Sibyl!" shouted Annie.

"Oh Annie! It's so good to have you back," a visibly excited Sibyl responded, "I didn't know how long you were going to be in the hole. The last five days have been terrible here all alone."

"Don't you worry about me Sibyl. I'm a big girl and can take care of myself. Now first things first, what unit does Hannah Jane live in?"

"Annie, I think you should leave well enough alone. I don't want to see you in the hole anymore on account of me."

"No, no, no. You have it all wrong. I'm not going to fight Hannah Jane. This time all I want to do is talk."

"Talk! Talk about what?" a clearly puzzled Sibyl replied.

"Hannah Jane and I have to clear the air between us so that we can both peacefully coexist for the duration of our respective sentences," responded Annie.

"Well if you want to talk to her you may want to arrange it through one of her friends."

"Any suggestions?" asked Annie.

"Try Patricia Golvan. She is Hannah Jane's right hand."

"Thanks Sibyl. I will. And don't worry. It'll simply be a peaceful powwow and nothing else."

Later that day out on the yard, Annie tracked down Patricia Golvan. "Hey Golvan! Do you have a minute?"

"What do you want Annie?" asked Patricia as she turned on her heels from the conversation with the other inmates.

"Just a minute to talk."

"About what?"

"I want to find out if you can set up a discrete meeting between Hannah Jane and me to bury the hatchet and end this ridiculous feud," said Annie so as not to reveal the true reason for the meeting.

"Discrete? What does that mean?"

"It means private."

"I can't promise you anything but I'll see what I can do Annie," said Patricia as she walked away. Now Annie had to wait and see if Hannah Jane was interested in learning the real reason for the meeting.

The next morning Annie awoke to Patricia standing outside her cell. "Hannah Jane says that there is nothing for the two of you to talk about," whispered Patricia, "and that the next time you two meet it'll be on like popcorn."

"So that's it?" responded Annie.

"Yeah, that's it," replied Patricia.

Now Annie realized that her master plan had taken a huge setback as a result of Hannah Jane's inability to get past her misdirected anger over Captain Draper. What could she do? Perhaps she would be able to carryout her plan all on her own. It seemed so difficult since she had only been at the prison for a short time with limited knowledge of its operation and limited number of friends, staff and inmate alike.

After a long day of kitchen duty, Annie finally got into the shower. She washed off the day's sweat, food, and cleaning solution. She daydreamed a little, as she always did in the shower, about her baby girl. In her daydream, she hugged and kissed Julia as the baby girl giggled. When Annie snapped out of it she realized she was still in prison. Unable to embrace Julia and listen to her little heart beat or watch her curiously observe what was going on around her. She knew at this point that her mother and baby as well as Sylvia, her attorney, probably had been turned away from the institution dozens of times with a myriad of excuses. She just wished there was a way to let them know what was taking place.

As Annie let the water run down her face, she was struck in the back of the head with a fist knocking her to the floor. As she looked up, Annie saw that she had been surrounded by three inmates including Hannah Jane, Patricia, and another woman she didn't know. Appreciating the circumstances that she faced, Annie quickly rose to her feet to stand in front of the other women stark naked.

"I'm glad you changed your mind about talking to me. I have some important information to share with you about Captain Draper," Annie said in an effort to pique Hannah Jane's interest and stave off an impending attack by the three women circling her like vultures.

"What about Draper?" responded a cautious Hannah Jane. She watched as Annie turned off the water, got out of the shower, and walked into the change room.

Drying herself with a towel, Annie replied, "When I found out, I could hardly believe it to be true."

"Go ahead and spit it out," a visibly interested Hannah Jane retorted as she and her friends followed Annie into the change room.

"Well, first things first. What's in it for me? If I tell you, then there's no incentive in you and your comrades here leaving me alone" said Annie.

With no real information to share with Hannah Jane, a now fully dressed Annie saw an unsecured mop, empty bucket, and ringer in the corner of the change room. In a split second, she grabbed the ringer and bashed the unknown female inmate in the head with it knocking her to the ground. Patricia, attempting to intervene, was shoved by Annie and lost her footing in a pool of standing water resulting in her hitting her head on the ground and being knocked unconscious. In an instant, Hannah Jane and Annie squared off.

Annie knew that she was at a disadvantage as she had never really actively fought with anyone while Hannah Jane had a well known reputation for beating the living shit out of other women. Annie felt a rush of adrenaline course through her excitedly nervous body. Perhaps it was her body trying to fend off the flood of fear Annie consciously felt. The mixture of adrenaline and nervousness made her reflexes a little quicker and her a little braver than she probably would be normally. However, she did have an advantage, which was her relatively high pain threshold from nearly two years of being beaten by Billy. As both women peered at one another, Annie tried to reason with Hannah Jane.

"Listen to me, Hannah Jane. There's nothing

going on between Captain Draper and me. In fact, he and all of the rest of the staff at this prison are taking advantage of us...using us," declared Annie in a labored voice as if anticipating having to fight her off. Annie began to panic a little but was ready to stand her ground.

Without a word, Hannah Jane lunged toward Annie in an attempt to grab her but Annie quickly dodged her. Now the entire scene had become a cat-and-mouse chase with Hannah Jane continuously attempting to ensnare Annie to no avail. When Hannah Jane finally got a hold of Annie, Annie proceeded to wildly punch and slap away at her. The two women wound up on the floor wrestling around as both attempted to get a hold of the other. Eventually, Annie got Hannah Jane into a headlock after receiving two or three solid fist blows to the back of the head from Hannah Jane that made her feel dazed. She started punching Annie in her left side in an effort to weaken her grip but Annie hung on for dear life despite the pain shooting through her.

With the fight appearing to be at a stalemate as Annie trying to maintain her grip, Sibyl walked into the change room all set to get into the shower. "My goodness what...what happened here? What are you two doing?" a surprised Sibyl said as she observed the two other inmates lying on the floor and Annie and Hannah Jane locked together.

"I was just taking a shower when these three idiots caught me unawares," said a visibly exhausted Annie.

"Well, you two need to stop this before the

COs catch you," responded Sibyl.

"Sibyl please explain to Hannah Jane what Draper did to you?" asked Annie.

"Let me go you bitch," huffed an angry Hannah Jane.

"I can't talk about that Annie," replied Sibyl.

"You have to. Hannah Jane needs to hear it," said Annie.

Clearly beginning to well up into tears, Sibyl responded "I can't talk about it. I don't want to relive it."

Hearing that, Annie's grip on Hannah Jane slowly began to loosen and Annie picked herself up off the floor and went to Sibyl and embraced her as Hannah Jane looked on still sprawled out on the floor.

"I'm so sorry for asking you to do that. I'm sorry for being so selfish Sibyl," said Annie, who was clearly disturbed by the fact that she asked Sibyl to do such a thing. Now sitting up trying to regain her breath, Hannah Jane saw from what was happening right in front of her that it was true. Captain Draper had been engaged in sexual acts with other female inmates in the prison. In fact, he was the initiator of those sexual acts. Now she understood why Annie wanted to talk to her. But she didn't know everything.

"So this is what you wanted me to know about Doyle?" asked Hannah Jane.

"Yes, that's part of what I wanted to talk to you about," replied Annie.

"What else is there? Did he do the same thing to you?" asked a now curious and angry Hannah Jane as struggled to pull herself together.

"No, but there was an attempt to coerce me into doing it," said Annie.

"What's it to you that Draper has screwed Sibyl?" inquired Hannah Jane.

"Shut your mouth bitch," shouted Sibyl. "Your boyfriend is a fucking rapist."

"I didn't mean it that way. Don't be so sensitive," said Hannah Jane.

"Let's stay on task girls. Sibyl is my friend. She's probably my best friend in the whole world. Anyhow, I sent a letter to my attorney in an effort to let her know about what had happened to Sibyl to see if she could help us," Annie said, "but Draper and his goons intercepted the letter and then tried to break me. I think part of it was to imply, through the grapevine, that he and I had been intimate when that was far from the truth."

"Damn girl! I should have listened to you when you told me that Draper had come on to you," said a clearly upset Hannah Jane. "I feel so damned stupid for believing his bullshit. I want to cut that motherfucker's throat."

"Well, I understand how you feel. What's more important is what we're going to do about these scumbags taking advantage of us and all the other women in this prison," responded Annie.

"I want to kill that son of bitch Draper. I feel like a complete idiot. I gave him my heart...my love," cried Hannah Jane.

"Killing him is not the solution," chimed in Annie.

"I'm open to suggestions," replied Hannah Jane.

"We need to make sure he ends up on the other side of these bars," emphasized Annie.

With that, Hannah Jane asked her now conscious cohorts to leave so that she, Sibyl, and Annie could talk privately. Annie began laying out her proposed solution to their mutual problem. Hannah Jane and Sibyl both listened intently as a whispering Annie systematically explained their path to freedom; freedom from rape, freedom from manipulation, and freedom from being treated like pieces of meat.

CHAPTER 22

The next night at about 8:30 p.m., Hannah Jane approached the security booth located in the center of her living unit. The booth was occupied by Sergeant Soren. She knocked on the window. Soren called out over the public address system, "What do you want Hannah Jane?"

"I just stopped by to see you."

"For what?"

Hannah Jane responded by flashing her bra and a smile to Sergeant Soren. In an instant, he buzzed her into the booth. Once inside the booth, Hannah Jane immediately removed her shirt exposing her state-issued bra.

Annie and two other female inmates, who had participated in the attack on her the other day, walked down a corridor being escorted by two male COs to Captain Draper's office. When they arrived at the office, Captain Draper hurriedly invited them in as he had received Annie's earlier kite. "So you have had a change of heart I see," chided Captain Draper.

"Well, I'm only going to do this if you promise me full protection and privileges in this place," replied Annie.

"You got it. You can have whatever you want as long as I'm here," said a visibly excited Captain Draper.

"I just want you to know not to expect this every time. I've never been with another woman before and probably will never do it again," explained Annie.

"I understand that and accept your terms. I've been waiting to get my hands on you for a long time. A woman like you can't be taken against her will. I want you to give yourself to me."

The two other prisoners walk over to Captain Draper and start rubbing his chest and clothed semi-hard cock. One of the inmates knelt in front of him and started undoing his pants and pulling them down as Annie began to slowly unbutton her shirt as she danced sensually. The kneeling inmate started to voraciously suck Captain Draper's cock, which caused him to toss his head back. Annie quickly grabbed the wooden baseball bat hanging on the wall and hit him over the head knocking him unconscious.

The three women then froze in place and listened intently to make sure no one outside had heard the large thud as Captain Draper hit the floor. As Annie and her two cohorts began searching the office, Hannah Jane's efforts were now in full swing. When she entered the booth, she had placed a large wad of gum on the lock preventing it from closing completely. Sergeant Soren began shedding his clothes while watching Hannah Jane masturbate with her hands down her pants.

As soon as he was stark naked, six women burst into the control booth and began beating Sergeant Soren about the head with various makeshift weapons including bars of soap in pillow cases. The tumult went on for about ten minutes as he attempted to fight the women off but it was rather hard to do as the women kicked and punched at his cock and balls. Eventually the women were able to subdue him. They used sheets to tie him up. This very scenario was playing out in the other three living units at the prison as Hannah Jane, well respected among the inmate population, convinced dozens of other women to join the plan. Their plan was nearly guaranteed to be a success as the female prisoners used male CO's kryptonite, sex, to gain access to out of bounds parts of the institution.

Back in Captain Draper's office, the women had tied the unconscious Captain to an exposed pipe running down the wall. First, Annie went through his pockets. She located a set of keys, a couple of condoms, and a pocket knife. She placed the pocket knife in her bra. Using the keys, Annie unlocked every file cabinet and drawer in the office and directed the other women to begin searching them. The women started ransacking Captain Draper's office searching for anything useful that they could get their hands on. Annie and the other women located keys to the armory and master keys to all of the access points. They found a set of uniforms. Additionally, in one file drawer there were hundreds of seized letters from friends and relatives of the inmates as well as those from the inmates to their loved ones.

"Annie, you gotta see this," said one of the female inmates.

"Take whatever you find that's useful and forget the rest," said Annie as she continued to go through a desk drawer.

"No, you need to see it," replied the female inmate.

"Okay, what's..." said Annie as she turned and noticed the desk was filled with letters. Annie began to cry as she started to quickly go through the letters searching for one from her mother with maybe a picture of her baby Julia. Finally, she came across one with her mother's name emblazoned in the upper left hand corner of the envelope. She slowed down at the sight of the letter.

"Go ahead, Annie. Open it," said one of the female inmates.

"We don't have time to..." Annie said trying to hold back her tears.

"Open it, Annie," the other female inmate repeated.

Annie began tugging at the sealed flap of the envelope until it tore open to reveal a letter written by her mother along with a picture of Julia. Looking at the picture, Annie began to smile. Turning her attention to the letter, she read that all was well with Julia and not to worry. She also read that her mother had attempted to visit her on numerous occasions but had been turned away with the excuse that Annie was in Segregation for violating prison rules. After finishing the letter, Annie searched feverishly for other correspondence from her mother. Her heart raced as if it were about to burst. She happened upon another letter and it appeared to be from Sylvia. Before she could open it, one of her fellow inmates reminded her to call the other units.

"Okay, what happened to the other COs in this building?" asked Annie.

"We only located six of them but we have locked them up."

"Alright," Annie got Draper's radio off of the desk. "This is Annie Lone. We have secured Draper, Administration, and the Armory. Over."

"Good job Annie. This is Hannah Jane. We have the Puget Unit. Over."

"The Alpine Unit is secured. Over."

"This is Susan here in the Palouse Unit. We kicked their asses. Over."

Annie and her two assistants then waited. They waited to hear from the last living unit. Had these women been successful in taking control?

Annie's mind raced about the possibilities; the possibility that the COs had gotten wind of their *secret* plot to seize the institution and called for outside assistance. If there had been a snitch amongst those inmates that Hannah Jane trusted, their plan may well fail. The plan depended heavily upon the women taking the entire institution. They had a substantial portion of the institution but they needed full control. They needed to be able to thwart any attempt by the FBI and/or the Washington State Patrol's SWAT Units from gaining entry through some weak point.

CHAPTER 23

CO James Toril took a sip from his coffee mug as he sat in Tower 1 overlooking the perimeter fences and razor wire with a spectacular view of Mount Baker. He heard a woman named Annie say they have Draper. Then he heard three other inmates call out over staff radios that living units had been seized. He nearly fell out of his chair as he sprang to his feet and grabbed his state-issued rifle. He peered out at the fences. He looked back inside the institution's perimeter and everything appeared to be calm. Simultaneously, Towers 2, 3, and 4 contacted one another over the radio to confirm what they had heard.

CO Toril said, "We better get off these radios because these inmates can hear everything we're saying. Over."

The radios fell silent as the Tower COs heeded

Toril's warning.

The two patrolling perimeter COs meet up.

"Toril's right. What the fuck is going on in there?" asked CO Ralph Crease.

"I don't know but whatever it is isn't good," responded CO Isla Latice.

"Well, it appears they don't have control of the Columbia Unit. Maybe we can get inside there."

"Yeah, but it could be dangerous if there was a failed takeover attempt and part of the unit is in the control of the inmates."

"That's a good point, Latice."

"We should call the Tower Officers and meet up."

CO Toril frantically grabbed manuals and binders off of the little shelf in the tower hurriedly flipping through dozens of pages. He came to a page labeled "Inmate Disturbances." After a quick read through he realized that he had to get on the red telephone and notify the Headquarters Duty Officer of the situation. Toril grabbed for the phone. It immediately began ringing.

"Hello, this is the duty officer," declared Correctional Manager Bruce Aaron in a sleepy voice.

"Sir MBCCW has been taken over. We have a riot situation," CO Toril said hastily.

"What happened?" asked Bruce.

"I don't know. I'm manning Tower 1. What I do know is that at least three of the Living Units and Administration have been taken."

"Well, looks like you're in charge. Get on the radio and get the available staff organized, notify the Whatcom County Sheriff's Office, State Patrol, and any other law enforcement agencies that you need assistance, and I'll wake up the Executive Management team and get them up to speed."

A crackle on the radio grabs CO Toril's attention.

"Sir someone is on the radio. Hold on," says CO Toril.

"The Columbia Unit is secured."

"Sir, it appears that all four Living Units are under the control of the inmates. The radios aren't safe. The inmates are using them. They can hear everything we say."

"Damn! Okay. Okay. Use them one last time to get the available staff together but then stay off of them."

"Yes sir."

"This is CO Isla Latice on perimeter patrol to the Perimeter Towers. Over."

"This is Tower 1. We need to meet up to talk at my tower. To the other Towers maintain your position; we'll have someone come talk to you. To any staff that can hear this, meet me at Tower 1. Now let's maintain radio silence. Over."

"We should take both perimeter vehicles to Tower 1. We'll probably need them to get around quickly," said CO Latice.

"Okay," replied CO Crease. Both officers got into their vehicles and headed toward Tower 1.

CHAPTER 24

Sticking to the plan, each of the living unit's leaders appointed a runner to come to Draper's Office to get instructions from Annie on how to proceed. The four runners arrived with three inmates escorting each of them. They arrived outside Draper's Office while Annie stood waiting for them.

"Hi ladies. Looks like everything is going smoothly. I need one of you from each unit to stay here to assist us with controlling this building. Any volunteers?" asked Annie.

The women from each unit have a brief discussion among themselves and four volunteers step forward.

"Alright! Now, find something to carry things in. We're going to the Armory. I'm going to hand out some batons, OC Spray, and flex cuffs to control the COs. When you get back to your units tell your leaders that they are to go through each unit to locate any staff that are hiding," Annie said. "I'll also issue some guns to those of you on escort teams to move about the institution."

"When are we going to contact the outside world?" queried one of the inmates.

"Soon, very soon. We'll tell the world about these sick perverts. But first we have to secure this place," responded Annie.

The women followed Annie to the Armory where she used Captain Draper's keys to access the weapons inside. While she only issued a few guns, she made sure that each unit had plenty of batons, flex cuffs, and OC Spray. With all unit runners well supplied she returned to Draper's office as they set off to arm their living unit.

CHAPTER 25

With all of the living units fully secured, Hannah Jane gathered a group of inmates to assist her in completing the takeover of the prison.

"Alright ladies! It's time for us to own this fucking place," exclaimed Hannah Jane. "We're going to go from building-to-building to make sure no staff members can hide and pose a risk to our success. Does anybody have any questions?"

Hannah Jane was extremely anxious and wanted to get moving quickly. It took her some negotiating but Annie had finally agreed that someone should secure all buildings in the prison compound lest they be used as a staging ground for an attempt to retake the prison by hiding COs. Secretly, however, Hannah Jane had an ulterior motive. She had been mistreated and disrespected her whole life. She wanted to regain her self-respect. She wanted to be respected. That's all she wanted in life now. Nothing more, nothing less.

"Jill, I want to leave you in charge of this unit. You guys just stick to the plan. Okay?" said Hannah Jane.

"Okay," replied Jill who watched as Hannah Jane used the COs keys to exit the unit.

CHAPTER 26

At about midnight, the Department of Corrections' Emergency Operations Center bustled with staff setting up computers, drafting proposed press releases, reviewing maps and diagrams of MBCCW, and contacting law enforcement partners from other state and local agencies for assistance; all under the watchful of eye of Prisons Deputy Secretary Russ Noblise. Russ had worked for Corrections for nearly thirty-six years in various roles starting as a CO and working his way up through the ranks into management.

However, he was not your stereotypical CO. Russ enjoyed listening to classical music rather than country. He would rather spend the weekend painting in his study as opposed to bagging a buck in the forest. Russ is what some would call a civilized warrior. His chosen profession was a savage enterprise; a savage enterprise that required warriors willing to do battle with societies worst individuals. You know, the people who don't act like people but instead act like wild animals in society and in prison.

Despite the popular belief advanced by the media and other various idiots in American society, inmates don't simply sit around and watch television all day. Many inmates are engaged in far more nefarious activities behind America's prison walls and Russ was well aware of that fact. They are organized in race-based criminal gangs that order hits on those rival gang members who have disrespected them. They often attempt to have unscrupulous corrections employees or inmates' own family and friends smuggle in everything from drugs, to cell phones, to guns. Weaker inmates are preyed upon by the stronger inmates for sexual gratification and dominance; mostly dominance.

This all takes place despite the litany of prison rules that have been drafted to prevent these activities. To enforce these rules, it requires warriors; warriors willing to deal with the threat of inmates throwing cocktails of feces, urine, blood, and/or vomit on them, warriors willing to cuff an HIV/AIDS or Hepatitis positive inmate who is spiting blood-filled saliva at them, warriors who may be the target of a criminal gang hit for enforcing prison rules or for some perceived act of disrespect. This was Russ Noblise's world. So when he received the telephone call that MBCCW had been taken in a riot he didn't panic. Russ rose from his bed and expeditiously dressed himself in preparation for the next battle of his long career.

"Russ, should we wake Secretary James?" asked the Communications Liaison.

"Of course! Just let him know that everything is under control. We haven't had any communications with the rioters. The entire institution appears to be under their control. And that the rioters are organized. We won't notify any media outlets until we have more information. Once we get our people on the ground in place we'll attempt to contact the inmates. Oh, and remind him that Superintendent Loons is in Australia on her Outback vacation," explained Russ.

"Will do," replied the Communications Liaison who immediately began dialing a telephone number on one of red telephones sitting in the middle of the table in the Emergency Operations Center.

CHAPTER 27

Annie stood in the hallway of the Administration building as the leaders of the units strolled in for their meeting. Many of the women looked exceedingly tired as it was almost one in the morning.

"Ladies, let's get this thing started," Annie spoke loudly. "The first thing we have to take care of is what our message will be, which media outlets to contact, and who will be our spokeswoman."

"Annie, I think we need national coverage and we should contact the big guns. You know CNN and MSNBC," explained Hannah Jane.

"I agree. We should also contact the Seattle Times and the Associated Press," added Jan.

"I thought this would be an easy decision. Now what will our message be to the rest of America?" asked Annie.

"I've been here for fifteen years and this has been going on for longer than I can remember. When I first got here I was nineteen years old. I had killed my dad one night when I was high on heroine after I started thinking about the way he molested my sister. I know I deserve to be here but I didn't deserve to be forced to give every CO on the third watch a blowjob," said Rita.

"Beyond our own experiences, we need to gather some other evidence of what has been going on here," interjected Carol, "because we all know that they'll say we're liars and manipulators. I know that Annie and her team searched Draper's office but we need to interrogate the staff we have captured to find out what else may be hidden in this place."

"You're right Carol. We need irrefutable proof. These are the stories we have to get out and any proof we get will make it a slam dunk. Rita, I take it that you're volunteering to participate in our media discussions?" queried Annie.

"I don't know what 'irref'...whatever means but no doubt about it you can count me in," responded Rita.

After getting several other volunteers willing to talk about the abuse they endured at MBCCW. Annie changed the subject one last time.

"The final thing we need to discuss is who'll be our spokeswoman?" asked Annie.

"The choice is easy for me. You should do it Annie," said Sibyl.

"Let's not jump at the first nomination. Anyone else interested?" queried Annie.

"Sibyl's right. You're the right woman for the job Annie," exclaimed Jan.

Rita jumped on board, "Exactly! You're a well-spoken, college-educated woman who would make us all proud and represent us good."

Hannah Jane stood up with a look of seriousness on her face and walked over to Annie.

"You've got to do this for us. You taught us how to stand up for ourselves and not be servants to these assholes. Don't try to abandon us now," Hannah Jane said as a tremendous smile overtook her feigned attempt at seriousness. She gave Annie a great big hug, which caused the other women in the room to gather around to do the same. Annie felt a great sense of pride after having brought the women together for a common purpose.

CHAPTER 28

"So far the State Patrol and the Whatcom County Sheriff's Office have setup a secure perimeter around the prison to prevent any escapes and established communications with the COs who are inside the perimeter fence," Russ said into the telephone.

"Any word from the rioters?" asked Secretary James.

"No not yet," replied Russ, "but the Incident Commander will have the Hostage Negotiators on scene soon and start the process."

"Good. We have to get an early handle on this situation. I'll be letting the Governor know what's going on. Have the Communications Office start preparing a press release for the media. Make sure the release lets them know we'll have regular updates of what's going on," said Secretary James.

"Yes sir. We'll stay on top of the situation," Russ responded.

"Do everything you can to end this thing quickly and safely. We don't need an Attica type situation on our hands."

"I agree."

Hanging up the phone Russ weighed the options ahead of him. He realized that he had limited options for ending the riot-turned-hostage taking peacefully. Either the inmates would surrender in a negotiated settlement or law enforcement would have to retake the prison by force.

CHAPTER 29

Inside the newly setup double-wide trailer just outside the prison's secure perimeter, Electronics Technicians from the Washington State Patrol completed the finishing touches on installing the computers and telephones needed for the command center to operate. The Hostage Negotiator, Sharon Planz, stood up from a table where she had just finished meeting with the negotiators from the State Patrol and the Whatcom County Sheriff's Office. They had received a situation report and developed a strategy for talking to the insurgent inmates. Walking to the bank of phones located at the other end of the trailer, Sharon picked one of them up and the telephone started ringing in the prison's Administration offices. It continued ringing for another three minutes.

"Well, it looks like the ladies are otherwise occupied," Sharon quipped. "We'll have to try this again a little later."

"Our helicopter with the forward looking infrared and heat imaging system is on its way from the Bellingham International Airport. We'll be able use it to see the location of the inmates in the prison, which will help us target the phones to call in on as well as assess where the inmates are congregating inside the prison," responded the State Patrol Liaison.

The prickly Sharon said, "Great! The sooner the better. We can find out what these degenerates want so we can wrap this thing up and get back home."

CHAPTER 30

The phone finally stopped ringing.

"You know, the next time we'll have to answer that and make up some lie to buy some time," said Sibyl.

"I know," replied Annie. "But first, we need to get the goods from these damned COs so that we have some ammunition. Starting with this piece of shit right here."

Annie was standing over the slowly awakening Captain Draper. She bent down and slapped him extremely hard across the face. Her slap was followed by a kick to the testicles from Sibyl.

"Wakeup you son-of-a-bitch, we have some fucking questions for you," Sibyl yelled to the now grimacing Captain Draper.

"Get the fuck away from me you whore," said Captain Draper.

"Motherfucker!" screamed Sibyl as she started hitting Captain Draper about the head and shoulders until Annie and several other inmates pulled her off of him.

"You know we could let her take you apart but we want to give you a chance to redeem yourself," said Annie.

"I ain't answering shit, bitch," replied Captain Draper. "You know, it's too bad I didn't get to enjoy that sweet piece of pussy of yours."
"I guess we'll just have to let Hannah Jane cut your rancid cock off then you…"

"You keep that nut job away from me."

"Why would we ever do that when you aren't giving us any incentive?"

"Fuck! What do you want to know?"

"Start by telling us where evidence is in this institution that proves what has been happening to us women."

"There isn't any."

"That's not true and you know it. Someone please get on the radio and get Hannah Jane over here from her unit." One inmate picked up one of the prison-issued radios and pressed the button but before she could say anything Captain Draper spoke up.

"There isn't anything at all."

"I'm sure Hannah Jane can find out for certain. Get her down here."

"Okay! Okay, just leave her out of this. If you go to the basement where archived records are stored you'll find several boxes of video recordings in a hidden room."

"If you're lying, we're going to lock you in a room alone with Hannah Jane and a couple of choice weapons."

"I'm not lying."

"Alright, I need you to give me directions on how to get there so that I can write it down and give it to our people to go and find the recordings."

"Okay Annie. Just keep Hannah Jane away from me."

After having written down the directions and removed Captain Draper's telephone and computer from his office, Annie and Sibyl left the office and locked the door to keep control of their high-value hostage. They met Patricia Golvan and Carol Plat outside of Draper's office.

"Annie, we *convinced* some of Draper's right hand men to share what they know about who above him knew about the rape factory they were running here. Well, you'll be glad to know that Superintendent Sarah Loons is completely in the dark about it," said Patricia.

"I don't know how glad I am about it but it's either a sign of incompetent aloofness or Draper and his cronies were running a slick covert operation," replied

Annie.

"I'm not sure it's entirely Draper's operation. It sounds like Associate Jennifer Welch was very much a part of this crime ring," added Carol.

"What the hell? She's the second woman I've found to know about this shit. How could she allow this shit to happen to another woman?" said Annie.

"The same way CO Rachel Soren stands by while her slime-ball husband Roy rapes women," continued Carol.

"Yeah, but it appears that Associate Welch never participated in any of it," Patricia said.

"Okay. This is all valuable intel that we can use. Sibyl and I learned from Draper that there are recordings of some of the heinous shit down in the basement. This is the evidence that we need to blow the lid off of this motherfucker if he's telling the truth. I would like to ask you two to come with me to the armory so that I can give you some weapons and grab three more ladies to go down to the basement to locate these recordings," asked Annie.

"For sure Annie," responded Carol.

"Definitely up for it," said Patricia. "We know how important it is to prove this because of the old adage that *all inmates are liars*. Hell, we may lie some of the time but we don't lie all the time."

"Alright! Let's go," Annie declared loudly as they all marched purposefully down the hall toward the weapons lockers.

Charles Malone

CHAPTER 31

"Are the SWAT Teams ready?" asked Russ via telephone.

"Yes, we have FBI, State Patrol, and the Whatcom County Sheriff's Office's SWAT Teams available in addition to our own Emergency Response Team (ERT) assembled here but they're still going over the prisons blueprints to coordinate any needed entry into the institution. Additionally, we haven't been able to raise the hostage takers over the phone and Sharon still wants to give it another try after the State Patrol's heat imaging and infrared helicopter arrives," said CO James Toril, the Incident Commander.

"If we can't end this peacefully don't hesitate to use the available teams to end this expeditiously. The Governor and the media are now aware of this incident."

"Oh, I won't."

"Keep me apprised of each escalation. If worse comes to worse, we may have to ask the Governor to call out the National Guard but I would like to avoid having to go that far."

"There are no obvious signs of violence being used inside the institution against our staff or other inmates."

"Good. But we need to find out what they're up to."

"As soon as we're able to raise the hostage takers over the phone we'll give you a full update on what we know."

"Has Jennifer arrived yet?"

"No not yet but when she arrives I'll relinquish the Incident Commander post to..."

"No you won't. You're doing a great job. If either of them has a question about it, just have them call me."

"Yes sir."

"Keep up the good work CO Toril."

CO Toril hung up the phone and started thinking intensely about the situation he faced. He had been a CO at DOC for nearly eleven years and this was the first time that so much responsibility was placed in his hands. It made him both nervous and enthusiastic about the opportunity to prove his mettle and intelligence.

CHAPTER 32

Patricia, Carol, and their helpers rolled a four-wheeled handcart down the hall toward Annie and several other inmates standing outside the Superintendent's Conference Room. The handcart was overloaded with twenty boxes.

"We hit pay dirt down there," huffed Carol. "These are all of the boxes that we could locate that contained videos."

Patricia added, "The son-of-a-bitches have a secret room down there that no one would find without having been there or having Draper's instructions. There was even a television set-up in the room with about eight chairs and a small refrigerator with beer in it. Want one?"

"Um, no thanks. These guys really are sick bastards," added Annie.

"Oh, that's not even the beginning of it. Those assholes have a mattress down there with a camera aimed at it along with boxes of condoms and sex toys," added Patricia.

"Let's see what's on these damn tapes," said Annie as she helped the women roll the handcart into the nearby conference room with the audio-video equipment. Noticing the boxes were labeled by month and year Annie looked for the most recent box. Once she located it, Annie started rooting through it at a rather frantic pace. She found a tape and stared at it for nearly a minute before going to the VCR to put it.

Once the tape started playing it showed a silent surveillance video recording of Jessica Wick in her cell. Jessica was a beautiful blonde nineteen-year old girl whose schizophrenic mind led her to commit the crime of arson in burning down her parent's home on Mercer Island. Her father had been one of Seattle's premier plaintiff's lawyers making a ton of money for himself but also for the clients he represented in medical malpractice suits against careless doctors. Her mother was a top notch surgeon at Seattle Medical Center.

She had the full support of her family but her mental illness overtook her causing her to run off on her own resulting in her parent's having her institutionalized each time except the last because she had become an adult and the police wouldn't look for her when her mother called them to assist the family in dealing with Jessica. Under the influence of her imbalanced mind, Jessica set fire to her parent's home and burned it to the ground believing that her parent's conspired with Russian agents to have her killed. That's how she landed at MBCCW.

Now to say that prison is not a place for a mentally ill person like Jessica was the understatement of the century. But Americans deal with their weakest, mentally speaking, by punishing them with prison sentences rather than helping them learn to live with their illnesses. The difference here is that Jessica had no idea that she faced torture in addition to punishment at MBCCW. In the video, four COs entered her cell as she sat on her bunk. Captain Doyle Draper and Lieutenant Lance Atron were among them. The mentally ill Jessica immediately responded by lunging toward the four men who didn't hesitate in using force to subdue her. As she lay unconscious on the floor, the men restrained her and carried her out of the cell and the video ended as other inmates poured into the conference room to watch the video.

Annie frantically rummaged through the box in search of another tape with the same date on it, which she quickly located. This tape had the additional label of "Juicy Jessica" on it, which caused Annie to wince upon seeing it. Annie placed it into the VCR and hit play. It showed the now conscious Jessica fully restrained along with four nearly naked men surrounding her; the same COs from the prior video. They took turns raping her and she began wailing like a wounded animal saying over-and-over again that she didn't have the information that they were looking for and begging them not to kill her. The COs laughed as it continued. Some stood around drinking beer while the others had their turn.

As the inmates in the conference room watched in utter horror, they realized that Jessica was still a virgin. Nearly all of the women were crying, some uncontrollably as they watched this girl suffer one of the most humiliating, degrading, and inhumane acts that one person can do to another; especially for a girl's first sexual experience.

Eventually, Captain Draper stepped back into the camera shot and started sexually assaulting Jessica again but this time he had a deranged look on his face. He took Jessica by the neck and began squeezing her throat with a force strong enough to cause her lips to start turning purple. Even then he didn't relent. In fact, he seemed more turned on by it. He continued his terrifically, horrendous assault until Jessica lost consciousness and control of her bladder. The other men in the room high-fived him as if he had just hit a home run. Not even acknowledging that he had just murdered a girl for nothing other than his own twisted desire for sexual gratification and violent control.

Some of the women watching began throwing up while others cried either hysterically or in soft whimpers. They cried because they remembered their own abuses. Abuses carried out by family friends, uncles, brothers, and fathers. In many instances, their mothers knew of the abuse but said nothing to the perpetrator either because of some public shame it may cause the family or fear of the abuser or, sometimes, blaming the victim because of the way she dressed, talked, or walked. No one had noticed that Hannah Jane had come into the conference room. She had also started to cry a soft, sorrowful cry. For anyone who knew Hannah Jane, they knew she never cried. She was tough, assertive, and abrasive. She was all those things but this tragedy brought something out of her.

This video had brought rushing back to her mind her own personal tragedy; the time her father and two of his drunk buddies forced her to perform all sorts of humiliating sexual acts when she was just fifteen years old. The man that she thought would protect her as a girl from evils like this had become one of her tormentors. She vividly remembered how her father's desertion of her in her time of need stripped her of any sense of security, calm, and self-esteem. Here she was again experiencing the same sense of abandonment by Doyle Draper as she watched him callously murder Jessica Wick. At that moment her mindset changed from one of following Annie's plan to one of vengeance. She wanted retribution for Jessica Wick, for Sibyl Enoch, and for any other girl who had suffered some similar vile abuse at the hands of Doyle Draper. Hannah Jane walked over to Annie.

"Give me the key to that room Annie," whispered Hannah Jane.

"No," replied Annie seeing the cold look in Hannah Jane's eyes. "What for?"

"Give me the key to that goddamn room," Hannah Jane loudly repeated.

"No!" responded Annie again.

"You're going to protect that murdering piece of shit in there?" asked Hannah Jane.

"No, I'm going to protect you. I'm going to protect you from receiving a capital conviction for murdering a motherfucker who is not worth your life," said Annie.

"Bullshit! Bullshit! Bullshit! Let me fucking end this miserable motherfucker's life now."

"I can't let you do that. Besides we have the evidence we need to get him sent to prison and believe me the male inmates won't be kind to him. He has a double whammy working against him. Not only is he a rapist-murderer of a teenage girl but he is also a hated CO. He doesn't stand a chance."

"I don't give a fuck. Give me..."

"Hannah Jane! Hannah Jane, let's go back to your unit," said Patricia Golvan as she took her by the wrist and led her out of the conference room.

"Ladies, I know how you all feel about watching what happened to Jessica but we need to get a measure of justice for Jessica by seeing to it that her attackers all face trial and conviction for what they did to her. Don't let what we've seen on that video take us off course. Look at those boxes there. We don't know how many other Jessicas there are out there. One thing that I can tell you is that we'll take every person involved in this atrocity down but we have to stick to our plan. It's nearly 4 a.m. Let's all try to get some shut eye for a bit," said Annie.

The women all nodded in unison as they all started leaving the conference room. Annie stood watching them with a ball of fear in the pit of her stomach that the loose alliance she had created with Hannah Jane may come unraveled.

CHAPTER 33

At about 4:30 in the morning, Sharon Planz sat at a table looking at heat image video taken by the State Patrol helicopter showing several dozen inmates inside the Administration Building. Then Sharon picked up her phone receiver and the telephone rang inside that very building.

"Hi this is Sharon..." Before she could finish her planned introduction she was cutoff and picked up a pen and started writing on a notepad. After writing for about two minutes, she hung up.

"Well, it appears we have a long list of demands from these ladies. They're willing to give up five hostages for each item on the list," said Sharon.

"What's on the list?" queried CO Toril.

"Oh, nothing except the Twilight DVD series, pizza and cheeseburgers for all the ladies, and access to the news media," replied Sharon.

"Why were you writing for so long?"

"Because they listed every media outlet, print, online, or televised, that they could think of."

"Did they mention anything about the message they want to convey to the media?"

"Nope. She just hung up the phone."

"Well at least we'll get fifteen staff out of there."

"The first two requests are okay and doable but do you want to give them access to the news media?" queried Sharon.

"You have a point. I'll have to get on the phone with Russ to get some guidance from him." As CO Toril made notes for his call to Russ, he grew a little relaxed as he saw a potential end in sight with this new development.

CHAPTER 34

At about 8 a.m., Sylvia sat behind her mahogany desk pounding away at the keys of her keyboard in an effort to finish the *Memorandum in Support of Plaintiff's Motion for Summary Judgment* that would be due to the court by 5 p.m. Her cell phone rang drawing a sigh from her lips.

"Hello, Sylvia Gray."

"Hi Sylvia. It's me Annie."

"Annie? Annie Lone?"

"Yes, it's me. I want to talk to you about something."

"What's going on up there?"

"That's what I want to talk to you about. We took over the institution."

"We? You participated in this?"

"Yes, I did."

"Annie, this could setback your efforts to get released on appeal."

"I understand Sylvia but things at this damned prison are out of control and dangerous for the inmates."

"How so?"

"Well, I can't go into detail over the phone now because I know they are probably monitoring all the lines out of the institution but needless to say there are crimes being committed almost daily here."

"Can you give me anything?"

"You'll know soon enough. What we need from you Sylvia is to get into contact with a federal prosecutor or even the state Attorney General's Office to help us. You'll know when because of the events that are soon to transpire here."

"I hope you're right about this Annie."

"I don't know if I am but we've got to do something to protect ourselves."

"Alright Annie, you can count on me. Just know that as your counselor I have to inform you that rioting and hostage taking are all crimes under state law. I'm advising you against participating in this and ask that you surrender."

"I know Sylvia. When it's all said and done

you'll see that it will have been all worth it."

Annie hung up the telephone and pondered her next move as the rest of the inmates prepared for the next phase of their plan.

CHAPTER 35

"Well, it sounds like most of their demands are fairly simple except the access to the media thing. We're going to have to come up with some way to delay responding to that one," said Russ.

"Sir, you should also know that we intercepted a call out of the institution to a lawyer named Sylvia Gray. Sylvia called the inmate Annie Lone. From reviewing the prison records there is an Annie Lone housed at Mount Baker on a murder conviction. She appears to be one of the leaders of the riot. More disturbing, however, she told this lawyer that crimes are being committed at MBCCW and that something was going to happen and that she needed her to react to it to assist them by talking to the U.S. Attorney's Office or the state Attorney General," CO Toril declared.

"Okay, first things first. Cutoff those damned

phones out of the prison. Secondly, I think that the request for access to the media may be related to their desire to make some kind of public statement. I have a plan to deal with that but first I need to get on the phone to the Secretary to get the clearance to go ahead with it. I'll call you back in a few to let you know how we'll deal with that but in the meantime get them the other stuff they requested."

"You got it." Russ hung up the phone and immediately started dialing another phone number as he considered the possibility that there was something going on at MBCCW that could seriously embarrass the Department of Corrections. He needed to seek counsel from his long time friend and boss.

"Hi Bob. We need to talk about the situation at Mount Baker," said Russ. As he updated Corrections Secretary Bob James, Russ wondered if there was any truth to the allegations that crimes were being committed and whether the inmates would trust anything he and the other prison administrators said as they tried to end the prison siege.

CHAPTER 36

"Hello," said Daryn.

"Hi mom. It's me, Annie."

"Oh Annie. It's so good to hear your voice. Every time I came up to that blasted prison they wouldn't let me see you because you were in segregation for some prison rule violation."

"I know mom but that's all a bunch of malarkey."

"Now I hear on the news that there was a riot and hostage taking at the prison. What's going on up there?"

"I don't want to go into that now. I just called to talk to Julia. Would you put her on the phone?"

"Of course dear. Hold on," said Daryn as she laid down the phone to retrieve the baby. "It's mommy on the phone." Daryn picked up the receiver and held it to Julia's ear while she sat on her lap.

"Hey baby girl. It's me mommy," said Annie with a crackling voice as she began to cry. All of a sudden the telephone line fell silent.

"Hello. Hello. You there mom?"

She had so much that she wanted to say to Julia but didn't have the chance to say it. Some of it amounted to nothing more that several dozen "I love yous" strung together like a tune. Some of it included an explanation for her absence from Julia's life. Surely the young child wouldn't understand it but Annie felt obligated to explain nevertheless. As she sat there holding the dead telephone receiver in her hand, she contemplated long and hard how to deal with the empty feeling she felt inside. Before she could become too engrossed in self-pity, Patricia Golvan approached her and tapped her on the shoulder snapping her out of her awkward abyss of pain.

"Annie, we're almost ready with everything," said Patricia.

"All of the equipment is setup too?" Annie asked.

"Yep," Patricia replied.

"Alright. Let's get it started," said Annie shifting her mental focus.

CHAPTER 37

After the phone line went dead, Daryn worried that something had happened to her daughter. She immediately picked up the phone and called Sylvia's personal cell phone.

"Hello," said Sylvia.

"I just got a call from Annie and the phone line all of a sudden went dead. What's going on up there? Is she a part of the riot?" Daryn queried.

"Is this Daryn?" asked Sylvia.

"Yes. Sorry for being so abrupt but I'm just worried about Annie."

"All that I know is that she mentioned something about crimes being committed at the prison and that she wanted me to pay attention to what happens and that I would know what to do."

"I saw the news and they mentioned gathering SWAT Teams for a possible assault on the prison to stop the riot."

"Yeah but they are bound to try to resolve the situation peacefully."

"I know but if something's going to happen that..."

"Daryn, don't put the cart before the horse. I don't believe that Annie is going to let things get that far. She's a smart woman. She'll figure a way out of this short of the SWAT Teams launching an attempt to retake the prison," said an unsure Sylvia attempting her best effort at comforting confidence.

"I hope you're right. I don't want anything to happen to her."

"Nor do I. So, I'll keep a watchful eye on the goings on at Mount Baker prison and as soon as something happens I'll spring into action."

"What are you going to do?"

"Well, I really don't know but Annie seems to think that I'll know exactly what to do at the right time. The only thing she was clear about was that she wanted me to contact a federal prosecutor."

"God, I hope she's right."

"This is probably a well thought out plan of hers. I say we sit tight and wait. Okay Daryn?"

"Okay Sylvia. Thank you for being so understanding."

"Anytime. I'll talk to you later. Goodbye."

"Goodbye." Daryn hung up the telephone and started thinking about what Sylvia had said. She wondered about Annie's plan. She hoped that it would be a peaceful resolution. As soon as she started thinking that it would be peaceful she started worrying about whether Annie's involvement would adversely affect her appeal. Worse yet, would Annie get more time tacked on to her already onerously long sentence.

CHAPTER 38

"Good evening America. We are broadcasting live here from our studios in Birmingham, Alabama. Welcome to the most trusted name in news, the U.S. News Network. I'm Chuck Greenlee here with Raquel Crisp. We have an exclusive news story for you tonight from the Mount Baker Corrections Center for Women near Bellingham, Washington, which is a town in northwestern Washington State just a short drive from the Canadian border. By now you've heard of the riot that has taken place at the prison. It has been under the control of the inmates for nearly a day and a half. Live via webcam, we have an inmate from inside the prison. Hello, what's your name?" asked Chuck Greenlee sitting next to his co-host Raquel Crisp.

"Annie. Annie Lone."

"Annie, what are you in prison for?"

"This interview is not about me. It's about

what's been going on at this prison."

"What's been going on at your prison?" asked Chuck.

"Crimes against the women housed here at Mount Baker. Your producer gave us an e-mail address and we've just uploaded some video and sent it to you a minute ago. Take a look at it. You'll get the point."

As the two anchors looked down at the screens just in front of them they saw the horrific footage of the rape of Jessica Wick. Chuck Greenlee was visibly disturbed by what he saw. Raquel Crisp grabbed her mouth and jumped to her feet as she began to vomit running out of camera shot.

"This...this happened at Mount Baker Corrections Center for Women to this young woman?" asked Chuck Greenlee as he attempted to compose himself.

"Yes it did. It happened to Jessica Wick. I'm sure her family was told she died by her own hand. But as you can see that's not at all true. Why don't you describe to America what you've just seen Mr. Greenlee."

"I just saw a young woman no older than twenty being violently raped by several naked men with what appears to be prison uniforms lying around."

"Mr. Greenlee we have boxes and boxes of videos containing evidence of sexual abuse that we uncovered here at Mount Baker. These are all evidence of their reign of terror over us."

"Were you a victim of these heinous prison guards?" Chuck asked tentatively.

"No, thank God. I had one of the men in the video that you just watched approach me but I rejected his advances and in return he put me in the Administrative Segregation Unit; your viewers probably know it as the hole. My friend was not so lucky. In fact, I walked in on her attack, which is how I first became aware of what was taking place at Mount Baker."

"Did you or your friend try to get help?"

"Yes, I wrote to my lawyer but the letters were being intercepted. I have some of my friends here who are willing to talk about their own experiences." The news segment went on for another forty-five minutes as she and her fellow inmates laid out details of the attacks on them or the attacks they had witnessed. Raquel eventually returned to her anchor chair but with a much less cheerful appearance on her face than when the broadcast began.

All of America's top television shows that night were ignored by the viewing public as they tuned in to listen to the crimes that had been taking place at Mount Baker. In the end, Annie made a plea for the FBI to send someone to the prison before the staff could retake it so that they could hand over the extensive evidence before the prison staff could destroy it.

Now the word was out as Annie had hoped. They had to wait and see what the FBI and the public would do to help them. Annie wondered to herself whether their tales of woe would be ignored as simply inmates exaggerating their plight or would the prison be comprehensively investigated by state or federal officials. How could they ignore such earth-shattering evidence? That night the ladies uploaded five additional videos demonstrating the atrocious actions of the Mount Baker prison administrators to the U.S. News Network to bolster their arguments.

CHAPTER 39

"Toril! Toril! Those damned inmates are on the air. Look at the television," shouted Sharon Planz pointing to the television.

"How in the world did they pull this off?" asked James Toril.

"Looks like they are using a webcam," replied Sharon.

"Turn it up," demanded CO Toril.

"Okay, but shouldn't we consider cutting the power to the institution?"

"I need to talk to headquarters about that but I don't think that it would be a good idea in the middle of the damn interview because it would look like we have something to hide. And how in the hell did they get a webcam in there in the first place?"

"Maybe the stuff they're alleging is true."

"Oh God, let's hope not," responded CO Toril as he turned his full attention to the interview while simultaneously dialing the number to Russ at Headquarters.

Charles Malone

CHAPTER 40

"Our Incident Commander, CO James Toril, made a wise decision not to cut power to the institution in the middle of the interview," said Russ speaking in a low voice into the telephone.

"Yeah but shouldn't he have cut the power sooner?" asked Secretary James.

"No, I would have done the same thing in his situation. The way the two anchors reacted at the sight of the video indicated that there may be some truth to what the women are alleging. We're recording the entire interview right now so that we can see what useful information can be pulled from it," responded Russ.

"I'm going to have to get on the phone with the Governor and explain what the hell's going on here. For all I know, I may well be asked to resign within the next hour or so. But that's not the concern at this time. What we need to do is figure out how to convince these women that we're sincere about wanting to protect them and investigate their complaints."

"Bob, I have a plan that may work but I need a little time to put it into action."

"Alright Russ. Go for it but make no mistake about it. If any of this is true. The Governor, the Feds, and who knows who else will be looking for their seven pounds of flesh in this thing. We're supposed to be protecting and rehabilitating these women. Not fucking them against their will."

"I understand. I'll do my best to convince them to stand down and that we're taking them serious."

"Has anyone been able to get a hold of Sarah Loons?"

"No she's completely unreachable. I guess cell phone reception is spotty in the Australian Outback."

"I thought so. One more thing. Try and get a copy of the other videos from the network to see what we're dealing with."

"Will do, boss."

"Ok."

"Ok. Talk to you later."

As Russ hung up the telephone he contemplated his incomplete plan carefully. Every detail had to be handled just right or it could spell disaster for everyone.

CHAPTER 41

Sylvia heard about the newscast from Imogene, her secretary, and had called her boyfriend to set his DVR to record it for her from the courthouse hallway. Now she sat on his couch mesmerized by the stories Annie and the other ladies of Mount Baker Corrections Center for Women were telling. As the interview went on, tears streamed from her eyes. Sylvia's boyfriend sat beside her and tried to comfort her. He placed his arms around her shoulders and pulled her close. Sylvia now fully understood what Annie wanted from her and she knew exactly what to do to get the ball rolling.

CHAPTER 42

Daryn caught the 10 p.m. rerun of the interview with Annie after having gotten the voicemail left by Sylvia's secretary later that night. She was stunned by the allegations of prison officials forcing the incarcerated women to perform sexual acts or face punishment. She was relieved, however, when Annie stated that she hadn't been attacked herself. Daryn knew that her daughter had already been through enough with Billy raping her and being separated from Julia. She didn't know how much more Annie could take.

However, she had learned from the interview that Annie had become a different person. Annie seemed confident, strong, and decisive. Daryn thought that maybe the separation from Julia had forced her to change. It had forced Annie to standup and fight for what she wanted. It had forced her to not be afraid. This was a good thing Daryn thought.

Annie wouldn't let fear rule her life anymore. The only lingering doubt in Daryn's mind was whether anyone would listen. She had read much about the way people in prison are little believed and often ignored. But maybe these video recordings would be forceful enough proof that the women at Mount Baker needed protection from the people that operated that prison.

CHAPTER 43

At just past midnight, Associate Superintendent Jennifer Welch arrived at the Incident Command Post and strode into the crowded trailer at the start of day three.

"What's going on here? I go up to Whistler to do a little snowboarding and people lose control of the damned place. Why are we allowing these women to get onto national television? Cut the power now," Jennifer demanded as she took a seat at the head of the table in the center of the room.

"No, that's not going to happen," responded CO Toril.

"Who do you think you're talking too? I'm the Associate Superintendent of this prison and you'll do what I say."

"Not right now, I won't. I'm under strict orders

from Headquarters to maintain my Incident Commander post."

"Who gave you that order?"

"Why does that matter to you?" added Sharon Planz. "All you need to know is that the order came from Headquarters."

Sharon and Jennifer had had a long and contentious working relationship in the Department of Corrections. They often had competed for the same jobs with Jennifer having the edge because of her long family connections in the Department and despite Sharon's greater skill and competence.

"You stay out of this Sharon," replied Jennifer.

"Listen Jennifer, you know damn well that the Incident Commander that's put in charge stays in charge for the duration of the incident unless replaced by HQ. But if you must know it was Deputy Secretary Russ Noblise who appointed Toril as the Incident Commander," sneered Sharon.

"Well that doesn't usurp my authority over this institution as Associate Superintendent."

"Ma'am, I'm certainly not trying to do that. I'm just following a direct order from HQ," added CO Toril.

"Well Incident Commander Toril, please give me a full debrief of the goings on up to this point and don't call me ma'am."

"Yes ma...Yes Associate Welch."

"That's better."

As CO Toril took a seat across the table from her, Jennifer had a growing knot in her stomach. The knot started off the size of a golf ball but grew to the size of a grapefruit as the thought of her involvement in the vile sex ring plagued her mind. She knew she needed to do something to cover her tracks.

CHAPTER 44

At about 9:30 a.m., Sylvia stood on the sidewalk in front of the Seattle Federal building that housed the United States District Court for the Western District of Washington with a gaggle of reporters gathered around her. Of course rain drizzled on the group as is usual in Western Washington for much of the year. Sylvia's hair had started to frizz but that was the last thing on her mind.

"Ladies and gentleman, I filed a class action lawsuit against the State of Washington, the Department of Corrections, Department of Corrections' Secretary Bob James, and several individuals to be named later after the criminal investigations have been concluded and all of the wrongdoers have been identified. The legal documents I filed today serve many purposes.

First, I filed an emergency *Motion for*

Preliminary Injunction to bar any retaliatory disciplinary proceedings against the women who ended the atrocious rape program operated by Mount Baker's prison staff as well as place the institution under the oversight of the court. The *Motion* also seeks to prevent the Department of Corrections and its officials from removing anything from the institution and, instead, have U.S. Marshals, FBI agents, or some other trusted and credible governmental entity enter the institution to gather evidence. Specifically, we want to ensure that the video recordings of criminal abuse are preserved as evidence. This evidence proves that the constitutional rights of dozens, if not hundreds, of female prison inmates have been violated. In particular, their Eighth Amendment right to be free from cruel and unusual punishments has been violated, which leads me to the other part of this lawsuit.

Secondly, we filed this class action lawsuit under the 42 U.S.C. § 1983, which authorizes injured parties to file lawsuits against state officials in their individual capacity who act under the color of law and violate an individual's constitutional rights. These women deserve to be compensated for the abuse they suffered. Whether they are identity thieves or murderers, no incarcerated woman deserves to be raped or coerced into sexual relations by the very people who are responsible for rehabilitating them. A class action lawsuit will allow us the latitude to identify all of the victims of this atrocity and attempt to make them whole. Thank you," said Sylvia as she concluded her brief remarks to the media scrum and turned to leave.

"Ms. Gray! Ms. Gray!" shouted several reporters.

"Okay, I have a couple of minutes for some questions," responded Sylvia.

"Ms. Gray, how did you come to represent these inmates?" asked a young male reporter for the *Bellingham Tribune*.

"Prior to this case I represented Annie Lone. The woman who revealed what was going on at Mount Baker Corrections Center for Women to America," replied Sylvia.

Another reporter from a Seattle radio station shouted, "Isn't she the woman who killed her sleeping husband in Thurston County?"

"She defended herself against a tyrannically violent woman abuser," added Sylvia. "Ultimately, she'll be vindicated on appeal."

"What's the likelihood of these women being successful in their lawsuit given the general impression of society that inmates lie all the time?" queried a young female reporter.

"You saw the face of the two reporters on the newscast last night? Once America sees what happened to these women, hell once I see what happened, you'll all be convinced and just as horrified, disgusted, and shocked as they were and understand that this cannot go on in America, a place where we cherish our constitutional rights and human dignity. I have no doubt that the court will grant our request for injunctive relief because it's clear that these women will face irreparable harm if the prison officials are allowed to resume their rape campaign. That's all I have to say."

"But you don't have any of the evidence to show to the court. Do you?" one of the journalists shouted as Sylvia was about to walk away.

"Not yet but I have signed declarations from the two journalists who watched the video that night as well as a copy of the video they watched. That's all I need."

As a tired Sylvia walked away from the gathered journalists, she felt a sense of accomplishment in conveying the message that Annie had hoped she would to America. Now she had to wait for a court to hear her *Motion for a Preliminary Injunction*. The success of the *Motion* was central to the success of the lawsuit. Sylvia also had a couple of other tricks up her sleeve.

CHAPTER 45

Annie and the other leaders of the revolt gathered in a conference room in the Administration Building at noon. The room was filled with a sense of accomplishment as the ladies jovially bantered about how they presented. Annie outwardly presented the façade of being upbeat but she was apprehensive. Her own experiences made her cautious. She internally lowered her expectations so that she wouldn't be disappointed with an adverse result.

She thought her defense in her criminal case would be a slam dunk but the jury's perception of reality proved a tough thing to overcome. But her emotions wouldn't let apprehension control her. She couldn't help but to feel a little satisfied with the success with which they had gotten their message out to America.

"Annie, you ready to get this thing started?"

asked Rita, the woman in charge of the Alpine Unit.

"Of course. Let's make it happen," responded Annie as she snapped out of her distracting thoughts. "Ladies! Ladies! We have some tough decisions to make now. First, what's our next step? Do we simply surrender the institution to the people outside or continue to hold it?"

"My vote is for us to hold it," snapped Patricia.

"I agree," added Carol, "I just got off the internet and saw that your lawyer Sylvia Gray filed some court documents on our behalf to protect us. We should wait to see the outcome."

"That's a bit of new news for us," said Annie as a smile broke across her lips, which triggered a similar reaction among the rest of the women, "I knew we could depend on Sylvia. Anyways, we have to keep in mind that the law enforcement officers gathering outside of this prison are planning for two scenarios. One involves a negotiated retaking of this prison. The other involves the use of force to retake this prison, which may involve gas, rubber bullets, and, possibly, real bullets. Knowing those realities, will we be able to maintain control long enough to await the outcome of the court proceedings?"

"Annie you always have to rain on our parade," added Hannah Jane.

"No, I just want to make sure that we fully understand and appreciate the downside to any decisions we make. That phone is going to ring again and we have to be able to tell their negotiators something to ensure that they continue to see the value of continued negotiations with us."

"I got it," said Susan. "We should offer up more hostages in exchange for things we need and set a timeline for our surrender. I saw it in a movie once."

"That could work," Hannah Jane declared.

"Of course it could," exclaimed Annie. "Alright, then we need to come up with what we want in exchange for these hostages."

"Let's just make sure that we keep Draper, the Sorens, and a few others who we know are the ringleaders of this," Hannah Jane quickly asserted.

"Definitely!" added Annie.

"I know no one wants to suggest this but what if Sylvia fails? Do we standup and fight any attempt to take control of this place?" asked Jan.

"Yeah, what do we do if she fails or if those cops outside get trigger happy and kills one of us?" Rita forcefully added. "I almost think that we arm ourselves now in preparation for a violent encounter with these pigs."

"Are you ready to die to day Rita? I'm not," chided Hannah Jane.

"I don't entirely disagree with Rita. We just have to make sure that we fully understand that any actions we take will have reverberating consequences as Hannah Jane points out and I like to try to consider the potential outcomes of what we do," Annie said.

"No doubt," declared Rita with an intense look

in Hannah Jane's direction.

"I have a suggestion. Let's take a bit of Susan's plan and Rita's plan. We negotiate hostages for something we want and setting a surrender timeline while simultaneously arming, training, and planning for an expected invasion force," joined the normally quite Sibyl. With that the women agreed and started piecing together a strategy and the various tactics needed to achieve it. Annie felt better about the decision in that the peaceful option had been given a chance.

CHAPTER 46

"Alright James, we have a plan here that may work at ending this thing peacefully. If the ladies accept our offer, we could have the team en route to Bellingham within the hour," said Russ.

"This seems like a really good idea. I think it may work," CO Toril said.

"The Governor's Chief of Staff certainly thinks so. They want us to make sure that the substance of the offer is not shared with anyone except you, the negotiator, and the women in the prison."

"Why's that?"

"The Governor's Office believes the women's stories and thinks that other staff members on scene may be implicated."

"Why are you sharing this with me?"

"We had HR look into your electronic personnel file and know that you haven't been at Mount Baker long. At least not long enough to have been invited into the secret circle of corruption that *may* exist up there."

"Thanks for the vote of confidence Russ."

"Don't thank me yet. We have to get these inmates to agree to the plan first. The key is that Sharon communicate this to them outside the presence of everyone except you. In addition to our concerns about the potential involvement of other Mount Baker staff, we don't need any background hecklers who may make the inmates question the sincerity of our offer and not accept it."

"Definitely. I'll get everyone out of this trailer and brief Sharon immediately."

"Good luck James."

"Thanks. I'll let you know as soon as we get a response from the inmates."

Jennifer watched James Toril hang up the telephone in the corner after having whispered as he talked to Russ Noblise for nearly thirty minutes. She wanted so bad to know what plan Russ had put together and how she could get involved to prevent herself from being implicated in what had taken place at Mount Baker.

CHAPTER 47

As Annie hung up the telephone after talking to the Hostage Negotiator Sharon Planz, she turned toward the rest of the ladies in the conference room with a huge smile on her face. "Guess what? They want to offer all of us immunity from prosecution under state law for the takeover of this prison," Annie said loudly. Cheers went up in the room. The room was filled with excitement and jovial chatter as the women realized that they may be on the verge of getting part of exactly what they were looking for.

"What do we have to do for it?" asked a skeptical Rita.

"Well, we have to allow a team from the state Office of the Attorney General into the institution to put us under oath and video record our statements of what happened here as it relates to the allegations of staff misconduct. In exchange, each person who gives a truthful statement will be offered a written offer of immunity from prosecution. She emphasized the *truthful* portion of the offer. I think that means if it is discovered that you didn't tell the truth the immunity is rescinded. So please ladies if we accept this offer, do not exaggerate what you know. Just tell the truth," explained Annie.

"What else do we have to do?" queried Susan.

"We also have to surrender Mount Baker to the officials outside of the institution within three hours of accepting the offer," Annie added.

"That time frame is unacceptable. How're they going to get all of our video testimony within three hours?" asked Rita.

"I think that they expect us to trust that they'll continue them after they are back in control," Annie replied.

"Well, I don't," added Rita.

"By the way, what about the prosecution of Draper and his minions? Do we get any guarantees of that? And what about all the video evidence we have here? How do we guarantee that it's properly handled by state employees who may just be trying to protect their own asses?" Jan asked.

"I can definitely ask for a longer time frame for us to surrender and request that the Attorney General conduct official investigations with the chief consideration of prosecution of Draper and his people. I don't think that he can guarantee a prosecution unless we provide the evidence," responded Annie.

"I would feel better if we handed over the video recordings to the Feds," said Rita.

"I agree. Yes our testimony is important but these videos are going to nail a bunch of these rapists' balls to the wall. If they could, they would destroy it as soon as they had the chance," said Hannah Jane.

"Okay, Okay. I'll respond to Sharon by saying we'll surrender the institution twenty-four hours after the Attorney General's team begins to record our testimony. I'll also ask that the FBI send in someone to take possession of the video recordings within that twenty-four hour period rather than state officials. Anything else?" Annie asked.

"Yeah. We should ask that the Attorney General's offer of immunity be reviewed by your lawyer. I think we should make sure that it's legit before we commit ourselves," said Rita. "You know they could try to trick us. When I got sent up, the cops tricked me into confessing."

"Agreed," Annie said as she started toward the telephone at the front of the conference room to convey the consensus of the group to Sharon. She was nervous but confident that they had a strong bargaining position. Once she got the phone in her hand the nervousness she felt suddenly grew because she knew that their success depended upon the outcome of this negotiation. She steadied herself emotionally before picking up the phone receiver.

CHAPTER 48

James stood at the sink washing his hands and staring in the mirror wondering if the women would agree to the offer he had Sharon convey to them. His success in handling this incident could mean a lot in the advancement of his career within the Department. He doused his face with the water running from the tap twice before grabbing a handful of paper towels to dry it.

"Hi James," a voice said. He looked over his shoulder and saw Jennifer Welch smiling at him as she turned the lock on the door. "You're doing a wonderful job as the Incident Commander."

"Thanks," replied CO Toril. "You can't be in here."

"I'll only be a minute. I just wanted to talk to you in private."

"Alright. What about?"

"About the plan."

"Oh! I...I'm not a liberty to talk about the plan."

"Okay. Was that from Russ?"

"He conveyed the message."

"The Secretary? Was it Secretary James?"

"I've said too much already," declared James as he tried to walk pass Jennifer. She simply stepped in his path preventing him from exiting the restroom. She started kissing his lips with soft sensual kisses causing him to pull back.

"What are you doing?" asked a stunned CO Toril.

"I just want to get to know you better," said Jennifer as she rubbed James' chest and slowly advanced down to his stomach until she reached his clothed cock, which began to harden and lengthen under her attentive hands.

"We shouldn't be doing this. Should we?"

"Just relax James," Jennifer replied as she knelt in front of James in her brown skirt and nylons. She unzipped his pants, reached in, and pulled out his semi-erect cock. "Wow. I bet the girls are pretty satisfied after you're done with them."

"I don't know about that."

"So modest...I like that in a guy."

After stroking his growing cock several times, Jennifer enveloped his length between her lips. As James' erection reached its full length, she slowly eased it out of her mouth and began working the full-length of it with her fist as she used her lips to massage and manipulate the head causing James to become weak in the knees requiring him to reach for the nearby wall so as not to fall to the floor. Eventually, she changed her method to trying to deep throat James' nine and a half inch cock. This caused James to cum deep inside her mouth, which only caused her to latch on tighter with her lips.

With Jennifer releasing her grip on his cock, James picked her up and kicked the trash receptacle onto its side. He laid her down on the side of it, pushed her skirt up around her waist, and began tugging at her panties and nylons. "It's time that I return the favor," CO Toril excitedly said.

"Here let me help you," Jennifer softly replied as she lifted her hips to allow him access to remove her nylons and panties. Once he had her panties in his hands, he hungrily tasted them before throwing them to the ground and devouring Jennifer's soaked crotch. In return, she grabbed his closely cropped brown hair in her fists and pulled him closer to her already smothered crotch. His oral ministrations eventually paid off as Jennifer started to climax.

"Put one of your fingers in my ass James. Please hurry."

Heeding her plea, James put an index finger inside Jennifer, which she immediately clenched tightly as wave after wave of gushing orgasm engulfed her.

"God, James you're so good. I need to feel you inside me right now."

After unbuttoning his pants and pushing them down, James stood up, picked Jennifer up off of the side of the trash receptacle, and impaled her on his erection. He held her steady as she threw her arms around his neck to hang on as he started plowing in and out of her slick hole.

After several minutes in that position, James put her down and bent her over the sink and pushed her skirt up around her waist. Jennifer looked at him in the mirror with a lustful gaze that signaled her approval as he reentered her. This time they both moved synchronously in slow rhythmic movements. Jennifer and James continued this way for the next five minutes as they locked eyes in the mirror as he unleashed his volley inside her with one final thrust.

The two remained in that position for a few moments as their excitement subsided. When James finally withdrew from her they both started getting dressed. James was a little uneasy about what had just happened as Jennifer was in his chain of command. They both would surely be investigated and disciplined if anyone found out. Of course, in a fair world she would receive a more severe disciplinary action because she was his superior and should have known better. But he knew that at the Department of Corrections, just like most public and private employers, discipline was handed out according to who had political power or who knew where the bodies were buried. James certainly knew that Jennifer had strong political connections within the Department, heck, probably within state government.

He simply couldn't resist her sexual overtures. Jennifer was a beautiful woman who, at age 48, still turned the heads of younger men.

Seeing the anxious look on James' face Jennifer said, "Hey, no one's going to find out. Not from me. We both have too much to lose."

"I...I'm glad to hear that," responded CO Toril.

"It's just good to have someone to connect with in that way. You know...no strings attached."

"Oh I agree."

"Well, maybe we can make this a regular thing. What do you think?" asked Jennifer as she retrieved her panties and put them back on.

"That would be great," replied CO Toril. "I have to be honest. I've never been with a woman as sophisticated as you. You're beautiful, smart, and know what you want. It's hard for a twenty-seven year old guy to meet women like you."

"Thanks for the complement." Sensing that she had gained James' trust, Jennifer popped the big question, "So what's next here in this operation?" With that question James now realized what had just happened to him. Standing in front of him was a beautiful woman with his DNA inside her who wanted to know information about the incident response that he was not at liberty to share with anyone. If he didn't give her this information, he stood the chance of feeling some retaliatory repercussions. If he did give her this information, he would surely be fired if anyone found out. He certainly knew at this juncture that he

had stepped in a steaming pile as he stood biting his
lip.

CHAPTER 49

Sharon Planz walked back into the Incident Command Center trailer and looked around. "Has anyone seen Toril or Associate Welch," she asked.

Everyone shook their heads and continued working. Sharon worried that Jennifer would try to sink her claws into James. Earlier in her career, Sharon had been a rising star within the Department of Corrections while working at the Willapa Bay Corrections Center (WBCC) in Pacific County, a male institution. Then Sharon was a Correctional Sergeant in charge of a shift. Jennifer was also a Correctional Sergeant.

Lieutenant Will Paup died suddenly and tragically in an accident while fishing on the Columbia River. His death devastated the tight-knit WBCC prison staff. He was not only popular but a nice guy who persuaded people to do what was right without exhorting to use of the power of his position. He and Sharon were particularly close. Will had been her mentor. They joined specialty teams at the prison and participated in more than one use of force quelling inmate fights or disturbances. Sharon had his back and he had hers.

When management posted Will Paup's now vacant Lieutenant position seeking interested applicants, most staff at the prison reflexively assumed that Sharon would definitely be the odds on favorite to get hired. After all, she was more than competent and worked hard to get herself prepared for the job. However, prison management hired Jennifer Welch as the Lieutenant. Rumors immediately began to swirl that Jennifer had spent time on her back to get the position. No one knew for sure but the way she operated around men in powerful positions suggested that she had put in the extra hours under many a sweaty overweight and balding upper prison management official.

Remembering this, Sharon was almost certain that Jennifer would be trying to manipulate CO Toril. Besides he was a half-decent looking guy, unlike many of her past conquests. While she thought James a competent man, he was just that, a man, who would be weak in the face of a beautiful woman with a warm, wet pussy at the offering. As she stood puzzling about what to do with the likely compromised James Toril, the telephone in front of her rang. "Hello, Mount Baker Incident Command, Planz here."

"We're on our way to the prison and are just a little lost on these county roads. Can you give us a little direction on how to get there?" asked a male voice.

"For sure," replied Sharon as she began to explain how to get to the prison in rural Whatcom County. She looked at the door hoping that James would walk through it after having successfully resisted Jennifer's slutty siren's song.

CHAPTER 50

James stood in front of the mirror as he contemplated Jennifer's question. His mind raced as he tried to come up with an answer for her. He wanted to be honest with her after what had just transpired between them but he couldn't unless he no longer wanted to work for the Department of Corrections. Not to mention telling her would violate his own high moral and ethical standards. Finally, he came up with something.

"Well, Jennifer, to tell you the truth, the plan is to allow the news media inside the institution to interview the women."

"What? Whose idea is that?"

"I...I'm afraid I've said too much already," said James as he unlocked the door and started to leave the restroom with Jennifer closely behind him. As they exited the restroom, four dark-colored cars pulled into the parking lot near the makeshift Incident Command Center. Several individuals dressed in suits exited their vehicles and started approaching the trailer with the sign that said *INCIDENT COMMAND CENTER*. CO Toril hurriedly approached the group to intercept them. Jennifer closely followed him. Sharon walked outside the door with a cigarette and lighter in her hand but stopped from lighting it upon seeing the strangers approaching the trailer and, instead, walked to meet them.

"Hi! I'm James Toril, the Incident Commander here," extending a hand to the guests.

"I'm Jonathan Goodnow. I'm an assistant attorney general. We brought twelve attorneys from our Complex Litigation Division along with three paralegals to assist in getting all of the statements officially recorded," as he shook hands with James, Sharon, and Jennifer.

Jennifer gave James a look of disappointment as she realized that he hadn't told her the truth about what the plan was for ending this inmate uprising. On the surface, she had the façade of a composed professional woman but inside she screamed. She cried. She realized that she was now likely to be implicated in this felonious scheme run by Captain Draper.

All sorts of crazy things ran through her mind. She could flee to a country that didn't have an extradition treaty with the United States. She could turn state's witness and cut a deal that might not result in prison time. After quickly pushing these plans out of her mind as implausible choices, she settled on a plan that would be extremely risky to her own safety but ultimately keep her name in the clear.

"Thanks for responding so quickly at the last minute," said James trying to push his thoughts about Jennifer's dissatisfaction with him lying to her out of his mind, focusing on the important task at hand.

"It's about time you guys got here. We're ready to get this damned thing done and over with," added Sharon.

"We still have to wait for the court reporters to arrive before we get started," replied a cautious AAG Goodnow. "From what we hear in the media, these inmates allege they have video proof of the alleged rapes. Is that at all possible?"

"You saw what we saw or, I guess, we didn't see on the primetime newscast," James answered.

"If I add my two cents, I think most of this is total B.S.," jumped in Jennifer.

"What's your role here?" AAG Goodnow asked Jennifer.

"I'm the Associate Superintendent of this prison."

"I thought that the prison management wouldn't be involved in managing this incident," asked AAG Goodnow.

"Don't worry. Mr. Toril is clearly in charge here," a testy Jennifer added as she shot another stronger look in James' direction. "Headquarters wanted to make sure that this incident was handled by a *neutral* person." Sharon smirked because it was obvious that Jennifer hadn't gotten anything out of CO Toril.

Sensing some tension in the air AAG Goodnow attempted to get back on track. "Let's hope this video footage is real or we'll have wasted a ton of resources responding to a bogus complaint."

"I'm sure we all agree with that sentiment," added CO Toril.

"Before you two start blowing each other and singing kumbaya, let's just not jump to conclusions that all the inmates are lying either here boys," Sharon abrasively said. AAG Goodnow recoiled at Sharon's comment.

"Yes but we don't want to have a public hanging of the suspected wrongdoers without evidence miss?" replied AAG Goodnow.

"Planz. Sharon Planz. I'm the negotiator here."

What no one knew was that AAG Goodnow had been the subject of a rape investigation when he was sixteen years old. Back in Michigan, he went to a party at a friend's house whose parents were out of town and drank so much beer that he could barely remember what happened except that he had run into one of the most popular girls at his school, Melanie Munford. She was in grade eleven and a cheerleader and, well, hot. She too had been drinking that night.

With alcohol fueling his courage, young Jonathan Goodnow strolled over to Melanie and began hitting on her. When she responded positively to his *moves*, he was shocked. He was even more shocked when she grabbed him and took him by his hand and led him upstairs. Remembering that the party host had asked partygoers not to go into his parent's bedroom, Melanie steered Jonathan toward the host's bedroom. Once inside, the teens pulled and tugged at one another's clothing until they were completely naked and engaged in sexual intercourse.

The next day the police showed up at Jonathan's house, handcuffed him, and took him to the police station based on rape allegations that Melanie was making against him. He tried to explain that she wanted to do it and, of course, the police responded that all rapists say the same thing. After the party host learned that Jonathan had been arrested, he wondered if they had been in his bedroom.

An hour later, he showed up at the police station with an exculpatory video from the recording devices he had secretly stashed in his room showing Melanie a free and willing participant in the sexual acts she and Jonathan engaged in. Now that he held the fate of others in his hands he wanted to make sure that a full and *fair* investigation took place before anyone would be hung out to dry as was almost the case for him so many years earlier.

"Alright, where do we setup?" he asked.

"This way. We got you guys some space over here," said CO Toril. As the group moved toward the location for the assistant attorneys general, everyone anxiously awaited the arrival of the court reporters to get started on documenting the evidence. However,

James' confidence grew as he thought he would be able to avoid any violent intervention to end the prison standoff.

CHAPTER 51

At 9 a.m. the next day, Sylvia stood in front of federal District Court Judge Sheldon O'Keefe set to begin her oral argument in support of the injunctive relief requested on behalf of the inmates at Mount Baker. Though she had argued in front of courts hundreds of times at this point in her career, she was more than a little bit nervous because the fate of these women hinged on her success here.

"Your honor, the state's response to our *Motion for a Preliminary Injunction* doesn't address the irreparable harm my clients face when the very individuals involved in violating their constitutional rights are likely to be put in charge of operating Mount Baker Corrections Center for Women when the state regains control of the institution. My clients are likely to be placed in the hole and face other retaliatory discipline because they exposed these criminal acts by the staff.

The video footage we submitted as Exhibit 1 clearly illustrates the end result of what the individuals in charge of that prison are capable of doing to these women. Jessica Wick didn't deserve to be raped, tortured, and murdered. Yes she was a convicted felon but she was also someone's daughter, sister, and friend. Even more, Jessica was a mentally ill person who needed help not abuse.

I can't emphasize enough to the court how much danger these women will be in if the state is allowed to resume control of this prison. In the horrific video footage, it is clear that Captain Doyle Draper is a participant in the crimes committed against Jessica. As the Captain at MBCCW, Mr. Draper is the head uniformed Corrections and Custody Officer in the prison. Who knows how many other uniformed staff and, for that matter, non-uniformed staff are involved in this crime syndicate," declared Sylvia.

After twenty minutes of argument on the *Motion*, she concluded and took her seat feeling a sense of accomplishment. Her mind raced. She wondered if she had missed any of the key points that she needed to emphasize. Overall, she felt satisfied with her performance.

However, it was now the state's turn to argue. The female assistant attorney general who appeared on behalf of the Department of Corrections and the State of Washington argued fervently and competently against the granting of the Preliminary Injunction. The young AAG had only been out of law school for a year and a half but she presented herself like a seasoned courtroom veteran.

She spoke of notions of federalism and the need for the federal courts to respect the authority of the states and their institutions. She even pulled out the tried and true <u>Turner v. Safley</u>, 482 U.S. 78 (1987) arguments where the Supreme Court of the United States adopted a deferential standard for state officials' actions in connection with the operation and administration of correctional facilities. To drive the point home, she pointed to the competence of the Washington State Patrol in investigating complex and controversial cases like the conservative state senator from rural eastern Washington who paid for sex with male prostitutes and sought reimbursement for it as an expense for carrying out his legislative duties. She also pointed to the statutory authority of the state Attorney General to prosecute crimes and that, if any of the allegations were found to be true, General Gage would surely enforce the laws of the state of Washington as he had sworn to do. Thirty-five minutes later she rested.

U.S. District Judge Sheldon O'Keefe offered Sylvia a chance to make a rebuttal argument but she didn't accept the offer except to say, "Your honor, I point out the state's failure to still address the very real danger my clients face of irreparable injury as a result of retaliatory actions that they could face by those facing prosecution." Sylvia sat back down and felt confident in her earlier argument. As Judge O'Keefe began addressing the courtroom, all eyes focused on his expressionless face when he started making his ruling. Though expressionless, his adept use of words mesmerized the courtroom as he drew the attention of all who could listen.

CHAPTER 52

Chuck Greenlee started the newscast with an air of excitement compared to his normally stiff persona that had become his trademark approach to presenting the news. "Tonight we have some idea of what will be taking place at Mount Baker Corrections Center for Women once the inmates surrender to authorities. Federal Judge Sheldon O'Keefe ordered that the prison not institute any new disciplinary proceedings against any inmates as well as ordered the state not to remove anything from the prison. Judge O'Keefe also ordered the U.S. Marshals to seize the video recordings and place them in evidence.

Those who observed Judge O'Keefe described him as uncharacteristically poignant and moving in his exposition of his ruling. The courtroom fell under a spell of eloquent prose something you wouldn't expect in a legal proceeding. I'm going to read a brief clip of what Jude O'Keefe said when handing down his ruling:

Charles Malone

'The rule of law protects
everyone regardless of their status in
our society. It doesn't vanish the day
you're convicted of a felony and sent to
prison. It cares not how evil of an act of
crime you committed to land yourself in
that prison. Rights are rights and these
women at Mount Baker Corrections
Center for Women have the right to be
protected. The right to be protected
from the vile and prurient sexual
exploitations visited upon them by
people we entrust with the
responsibility to make sure these
women serve their sentences safely.

Standing alone, what happened
to Jessica Wick in the video recording
submitted into evidence is sufficient
grounds to find an Eighth Amendment
violation. If there is evidence that other
women at Mount Baker were subjected
to rape and torture, then there is no
doubt that this court has an obligation
to intervene to prevent retaliation of
the kind that may lead to another
inmate's death as well as preserve the
evidence of those crimes. The rule of
law demands it and justice requires it.
These women have the right to their
dignity and bodily integrity and forcing
or coercing them to engage in sexual
acts destroys that to the detriment of
society and, most importantly, the
women whose self-worth and

confidence are destroyed because of the violent and selfish acts of another person.'

Man, Judge O'Keefe's exhortation on rights was powerful. What do you think Raquel?"

"Chuck, I agree. Judge O'Keefe assayed a full-throated defense of women's liberty in his forty minute ruling. Of course, the state says they are going to consider appealing the issuance of the Preliminary Injunction," declared Raquel. The newscast continued as Chuck and Raquel brought on a variety of legal analysts to discuss Judge O'Keefe's ruling.

Judge O'Keefe was appointed to the bench by President Ronald Reagan. He tended to have a conservative legal philosophy that deferred to government power. The appointment of a federal judge is a rather rigorous and political process that leaves few stones unturned in a judicial nominee's life. The FBI conducts extensive background checks on all potential nominees for the president of the United States. Opposing senators dig comprehensively through anything a nominee has written looking for ammunition to thwart the appointment. Not to mention the special interest groups who have a bone to pick with the nominees who go out of their way looking for mud to sling as the confirmation vote approaches. Needless to say, senatorially-confirmed nominees are well vetted before they take their seats on the federal bench.

However, one thing that never came up in Sheldon O'Keefe's confirmation hearing, though the FBI made note of it, was his sister being raped. Amber

O'Keefe was gang raped at the age of seventeen by a supposed boyfriend and two of his buddies and it destroyed her life. Sheldon, at the age of fifteen, proceeded to whip the living daylights out of the supposed boyfriend with his bare hands right in front of the Anniston, Alabama Police Department as he exited the jail. The boy was beaten so bad that he had a shattered eye socket and a broken nose. The police who stopped Sheldon's assault on the rapist felt compelled not to file a police report or do anything else, despite the protestations of the rapist-boyfriend's mother, because of the sheer brutality of what was done to Amber. Her son was eventually sent to prison along with his friends and Amber took her own life a year later. Sheldon never got over the loss of his sister.

CHAPTER 53

Later that night after Judge O'Keefe's ruling, the Emergency Response Team moved slowly and methodically toward the entrance of the prison's administration building with six secure metal containers on a four-wheeled dolly brought in by the U.S. Marshals. No one was quite sure how many of the containers were needed but the Marshals made sure there were more than enough. The silver containers were about three feet long, two feet wide, and two feet deep. The containers were for the video tapes the inmates discovered. The Marshals would take custody of the secure containers as required by Judge O'Keefe's court order.

The Marshals that arrived looked on as the team put the containers in place. Once all were in place, the Emergency Response Team withdrew as they had done in all previous exchanges with the inmates. Several inmates opened the door and began rolling the dolly into the Administration Building.

CHAPTER 54

Annie was sitting in a corner fast asleep at about 8 a.m. She was awakened by a commotion outside of the conference room. She quickly got to her feet, looked for her keys on the table, and discovered they were missing. Rushing into the hallway, Annie saw women standing outside the open door of Captain Draper's office. She panicked when she realized what was going on. When she reached the door her worst fears were confirmed. Draper was still secured to the exposed pipe but he had several fresh bruises and cuts to his face. A crying Hannah Jane was standing over him with a state-issued forty-five caliber handgun that she had taken from the armory using Annie's keys. Draper saw Annie.

"Annie, I thought you were going to keep her away from me," yelled a scared Captain Draper.

"Shut the fuck up you. Don't you say one damn

thing you lying sack of shit. How could you...kill that girl...lie to me?" said Hannah Jane trembling as she pointed the gun at Captain Draper's bloody face.

"Hannah Jane, don't do this," begged Annie. "Please, don't."

"Why not? I don't have anything else to live for. I don't have a little girl like you to go back to. All I had to look forward to was marrying Doyle here only to find out he lied to me and used me."

"Hannah Jane, there is that special someone out there for you. If you kill this son-of-a-bitch you'll never get to find him because you'll be locked up for the rest of your life."

"Annie's right, Hannah Jane. Don't do this," added Patricia Golvan. "I...I love you." When the words crossed her lips she knew that she couldn't take them back. She delivered those words in a way that a friend wouldn't. She delivered them in the way a person who romantically loved another person would; with true heartfelt emotion that inundated her voice. The cat was out of the bag, but she didn't care. All that mattered was that Hannah Jane knew exactly how she felt about her.

Hannah Jane froze for a minute. The two women had been close friends but nothing more. Patricia grew a little red with embarrassment for revealing so much of herself in front of everyone else. Hannah Jane's preference for men was clear to Patricia. So, she knew that Hannah Jane didn't feel romantic love for her but it didn't matter to her. People fell in love with other people who didn't feel the same way all the time. Patricia was not going to hold back her emotional adoration for Hannah Jane any longer. She wanted to liberate her emotion as opposed to bottling it up causing herself anguish. Patricia figured that her expression of love would not be returned but she simply didn't care how Hannah Jane would react to her emotional overture because this was about her own peace of mind.

"I love you too, Patricia. You've been a true friend to me all these years. I don't know how to repay you for it," Hannah Jane said as she lowered the gun. Patricia took Hannah Jane's hand into hers.

"Hannah Jane, just know that we're here for you," Annie whispered with tears in her eyes.

"The two of you are probably the first two to ever really care about me. God, I wish I had met you when I was a young woman when my hopes and dreams were still alive. When I still had a chance," said Hannah Jane.

"You talk like this is the end of the world. It's not," replied Annie as a loud crash was heard in the hallway. "It's only the beginning. Would someone see what that noise was?"

"I don't know. I just feel that this lying motherfucker will get away with murdering Jessica, lying to me, and the rapes of God-knows how many girls," said Hannah Jane.

"He won't Hannah Jane. He won't. We got the evidence to lock him up for a long time. Not to mention the fact that once he's locked up he'll have to watch his back everyday. Okay?" said Annie as she tried to comfort Hannah Jane's fears.

"You're right Annie," said Hannah Jane as she raised her arm to hand her gun to Annie. But before the exchange could occur, Jennifer Welch surprised everyone by moving through the crowd of women with a gun to the head of a young inmate named Ariel who was scared senseless. Hannah Jane immediately withdrew the gun and pointed it at Jennifer.

"Alright ladies, I thought you were going to take care of this for me but you had to do the *right thing*," a frustrated looking Jennifer said. "I guess if you want something done right you have to do it yourself." Jennifer continued to hold Ariel around the neck with the barrel of her gun flush to her skull.

"Help me guys," Ariel cried.

"Shut the fuck up," yelled Jennifer as she pushed the gun harder into Ariel's head. "Now un-cuff him and hand him over. And Hannah Jane, stop pointing that gun at me. It makes me nervous."

"No! Don't do it. You guys will be accessories to my murder," a frantic Captain Draper said.

"No they won't. They're going to be your murderers when I'm done here," responded Jennifer. "Now un-cuff his ass and give him to me."

"We're not going to do that," exclaimed Annie.

"Then you want to see this little bitch's brains all over the place."

"You won't do that. There are too many witnesses," Annie said.

"And if you shoot her, I'm going to shoot you bitch," added Hannah Jane. The standoff grew tenser as an unyielding Jennifer continued to demand the handover of Doyle Draper.

CHAPTER 55

James Toril came back into the Incident Command Center and quickly glanced around the room before taking a seat at the table to read some situation reports. Sharon got up from the table and walked over to James' end of the table and whispered, "You didn't tell Jennifer anything, did you because I haven't seen her in a while?"

"Well, I lied to her about the plan."

"What did you tell her?"

"It's more what didn't I tell her."

"So she was shocked to see the people from the AG's Office here. Hold on."

Feeling a bit unsettled about Jennifer's absence, Sharon walked over to the telephone used to communicate with the inmates and picked up the receiver. It started ringing. It continued to ring. After letting it ring for nearly two minutes, Sharon hung up and looked outside. Seeing Jennifer's car still parked in the parking lot she walked over to CO Toril and said, "I think we have our answer to where she is."

"How the…"

"She got in when the Emergency Response Team gave the inmates the secure boxes for the video tapes. That's the only way she could pull it off."

"Son-of-a-bitch! I need to call Russ," declared CO Toril as he grabbed the phone.

CHAPTER 56

"Nobody better answer that phone," said Jennifer.

"You're not going to get away with this," Annie responded.

"Shut up and hand over that asshole."

"They're probably looking for you out there right now," added Hannah Jane.

"I don't want to hear anything from you. Shut that cock hole on your face," Jennifer shouted as she became more agitated.

She began wildly pointing the gun at different people in the room while still maintaining a near chokehold on Ariel. Jennifer started realizing that the odds were stacked against her with all of these inmates present and slowing her down in the execution of what initially seemed like a solid plan. She thought that if she could get out of the prison quickly she could make up a story about her whereabouts. Now feeling the pressure she had begun to sweat heavily.

With resolve, she pointed her gun and pulled the trigger three times. The bullets exploded from the gun with precision striking Doyle Draper twice in the chest and once in the head. Everyone in the office and hallway hit the deck except Hannah Jane who stood her ground with the gun pointed at Jennifer trying to find a clear shot that wouldn't hit Ariel.

"I'm not going to kill you today, Hannah Jane," declared Jennifer. As Doyle sat mortally wounded against the wall, Jennifer continued to hold onto Ariel and slowly backed out of the office.

"Listen up little bitch. You're next if you don't tell me where to find the Sorens," demanded Jennifer. With tears streaming down her cheeks, the shaking Ariel pointed Jennifer in the right direction.

"I don't have time for this. Fucking show me the way," she said as she pressed the now hot gun barrel hard against Ariel's temple burning her. They walked down the hallway and reached the room where the Sorens were being held with other high value staff members. The women guarding the room were standing with their guns drawn after hearing the gunshots but seeing Ariel as a hostage they put down their weapons and held up their hands.

"That's right. I don't want to kill her but if you make me I have no qualms about doing this bitch.

Now unlock the damned door," chided Jennifer.

With the door opened, Jennifer went into the room dragging Ariel along and fired three shots; each hitting their intended targets in the head. She realized her luck when she saw Lance Atron in the room. She had no direct dealings with him but he had been Captain Draper's right hand man. Who knew what Doyle had told him? Because of that uncertainty, he had to die.

Once she came back out of the room with Ariel in tow the two inmates that had been guarding the room stayed there and had not picked up their guns. With that she shot and killed the two disarmed inmate-guards without warning upon exiting the room. By now, Ariel was hysterical.

"Please don't kill me!" cried Ariel.

"Come on. You were never going to amount to anything anyway," Jennifer said to a sobbing Ariel as she pushed her against the opposite wall. With those words she shot Ariel through the forehead and watched as her body hit the concrete floor with such force that it bounced.

Feeling comforted that she had achieved her goal; Jennifer started making her way to an exit. She was confident that no one would believe anything that any of the inmates in Draper's office would say. Now the final phase of her plan was in motion and she knew that its success depended on her quick departure. As she moved down the corridor to leave, Jennifer realized that she had made a huge mistake; an oversight that could cost her everything. She paused and had an important decision to make. Go back and risk being found out or continue moving ahead in hopes that the inmates had dropped the ball.

CHAPTER 57

The SWAT Teams and the DOC's Emergency Response Team quickly got their gear on. Team members were putting on bullet proof vests, checking their ammunition, and leaders were reviewing the prison's blueprints when they heard the first gunshots.

"What the fuck is going on in there?" shouted James to members of his Incident Command team.

Sharon responded "I'm going to find out," as she grabbed the telephone, which started ringing immediately.

"Hello," said a frantic voice.

"Who's this?" asked Sharon.

"This is Joan."

"Joan, what's going on in there?"

"Associate Superintendent Welch is shooting everybody."

"What? She did what?"

"She's shot a bunch of folks."

"Can you give me Annie?"

"Annie! Annie! This negotiator lady wants to talk to you," Joan yelled.

Annie took the phone from Joan. "You guys need to get some fucking ambulances here quick. We have seven people that have been shot," yelled Annie.

"Seven! By who?" queried Sharon.

"Does it matter? Jennifer. Just get some EMTs here quick," a scattered Annie responded and the phone went silent. The radio crackled and the Emergency Response Team informed James that the door to the Administration Building was opening. They saw several inmates exit the door carrying stretchers that were placed so that they could be picked up. Luckily they had two ambulances on standby, which were directed toward the stretchers where they found several people all ready dead from bullet wounds and some with very faint pulses, including Doyle Draper who was immediately transported to Bellingham General Hospital.

Watching the scene unfold, James was completely dumbfounded to learn that Jennifer had done this. He didn't realize that she was capable of murder. A clear indication of just how involved she had been in the allegations that had led to the prison riot in the first place. The proof being that four of the seven targets of her gunfire had been high-ranking prison staff. He knew he had to get on the phone with Russ to brief him before he heard about it in the media. He just didn't know how to break the news to him that Jennifer was the probable culprit behind it. While there was no direct evidence of her involvement, just inmates saying that she was involved, there was no sign of her around the Incident Command Center, which leant support to their allegations.

CHAPTER 58

Doyle Draper was in the Emergency Room on the gurney with two surgeons and the ER's attending physician trying to stop the bleeding from several wounds. His wife, Casey, and their two teenage sons, Paul and John, rushed into the ER and were shown to the Trauma Room where he was currently being worked on in an effort to stabilize his injuries to get him to the Operating Room. As soon as Casey saw her husband lying motionless with blood all over the floor, she collapsed only to be caught by her two boys.

She had been madly in love with Doyle for all of these years. In fact, they had been high school sweethearts. He had been a devoted father and husband; always finding the time to be there for those school plays, baseball games, and the boys' first breakups with their girlfriends. He had also been there for Casey in her time of need. When she lost her parents in tragic car accident four years ago Doyle had been her rock. He was everything that she wanted in a man and more.

Now he was vulnerable. She always knew that his job at Mount Baker had the potential for danger but it was a women's prison. How dangerous could that be? Female inmates don't walk around with shanks or ice picks.

"Doctor, is my husband going to be alright?" asked a crying Casey.

"Right now we're trying to stop the bleeding and get him up to the OR," replied the Chief of Surgery. "He's in good hands."

"Is he going to be okay? You can save him, right?" a crying Casey asked.

"He has some serious injuries. We have to get him upstairs to get a better look at them," responded the Chief of Surgery.

"How bad is it?" asked the oldest boy, Paul, who was nineteen.

"Your father has two gunshot wounds to the chest and one to the head. We're going to do all we can for him."

The three of them stood watching as the Chief of Surgery returned to the side of the gurney and led their father's still body out of the room and into an elevator. They had never seen him this vulnerable before. It scared them. He had tubes attached to both arms and one coming out of his chest. Fear was now their new unwanted companion along with uncertainty.

CHAPTER 59

"According to the inmates, Jennifer is responsible for all of this. It's like she snapped or something," exclaimed CO Toril.

"We can't get bogged down on why she did it. We have to stay focused on how to end this before more people get hurt," Russ responded. "Now we should consider sending in the SWAT teams and the Emergency Response Team to retake the prison. I have to get clearance from the Secretary."

"So in the meantime what should I do here? We haven't been able to locate Jennifer. We tried her cell several times with no luck."

"Any proof other than the inmates saying she did this."

"Isn't her absence from the scene enough?"

"I have to admit that it's a little suspicious but we can't prove anything right now. Let me talk to Secretary and get back to you."

"Alright Russ I'll stay close to the phone to get orders from you," ended James. He hung up the phone quickly and rushed to let the SWAT teams and Emergency Response Team know that they needed to be on standby for orders from the Governor to act immediately. James' anxiety was through the roof as he rushed to get the teams together. He stumbled on his way out the front door of the Incident Command Center nearly falling flat on his face as his mind was overwhelmed with the worry about what was going on inside the prison.

CHAPTER 60

Jennifer slowly made her way down the corridor back toward Doyle Draper's Office. She was trying to move as fast as she could but as she rounded a corner Patricia spotted her and Jennifer fired a shot in her direction before taking cover because Patricia raised her arm to aim her gun at Jennifer. The bullet grazed Patricia's cheek, which trickled blood down to her chin. Patricia returned fire at Jennifer as she, Hannah Jane, and two other armed inmates took cover behind an old desk that sat in the hallway that Hannah Jane turned over.

Patricia shouted, "What did you come back for? To kill the rest of us?"

"I just forgot something. I'm going to come and get it and then I'll leave."

"Drop dead you murdering bitch. You should get the hell out of here now," added Hannah Jane.

"Alright ladies hold your fire. We may need every last bullet in those guns because Associate Welch is a marksman. At least that's what I heard among her staff years ago," Patricia instructed the others.

"I'll be out of your hair in a matter of minutes," explained a frustrated Jennifer. "Just let me come get what I need." The inmates didn't respond to her proposed solution. Realizing that she could be in a standoff with these inmates for hours, she took a big risk and stood with the gun pointed in their direction and started moving toward them like a tiger that had zeroed in on some prey. At any moment any one of those inmates could poke their head out from behind the table and she would kill them with a precise shot to the forehead.

As expected, Patricia peaked up from behind the table and was surprised to see Jennifer coming at her at a quick pace. Patricia was immediately stricken with fear as she realized she could be killed at this very moment staring down the barrel of a gun. Jennifer pulled the trigger but in a split second Annie came out from behind the corner just to the left of the overturned desk and hit Jennifer's arm causing the bullet to strike a photograph of Superintendent Loons on the wall. Jennifer then began raising the gun to shoot Annie. Annie hit her arm again and punched Jennifer in the stomach. As the gun fell to the ground, Jennifer responded by delivering two blows to Annie's throat causing her to fall to her knees. Jennifer was a marksman but also a black belt in Shaolin karate. Annie couldn't breathe as she wreathed in pain on the floor holding her throat.

Jennifer retrieved her gun and stood over Annie. "Well, you put up the good fight. Too bad it wasn't good enough," smirked Jennifer. As she wreathed on the floor facedown in the fetal position, Annie thought about Julia. She had to make it out of this for her. She remembered the pocket knife she took off Captain Draper's desk. She reached into her bra and unfolded the knife. In one quick motion, she stabbed Jennifer in the ankle. The pain Jennifer felt was intense enough for Annie to grab Jennifer by both legs and push her down before she could squeeze the trigger. Annie then proceeded to put her oversized feet to good use by kicking Jennifer's hand over and over again in an effort to make her let go of the gun.

"Stop kicking me with those damned planks you bitch," shouted Jennifer. She got off three additional wild shots causing everyone within the vicinity to take cover behind the nearest obstacle. Eventually, Jennifer dropped the gun but Annie continued by sitting on her and punching her in the chest and face. From the blows she had received earlier, Annie realized that Jennifer could beat her ass on any given day and couldn't let her regain the advantage.

"Ladies, I need some help," Annie yelled as Jennifer clawed at her face and eyes, punched Annie's ribs and kidneys, as well as thrashed her body around in an effort to roll Annie off her. In a matter of seconds, Patricia, Hannah Jane, and several other inmates grabbed Jennifer by the arms and held her down.

"Anybody got some flex cuffs?" yelled Hannah Jane. Sibyl came over and handed her a pair, which were applied tightly to Jennifer's wrists.

"You bitches are going to ruin my career," shouted Jennifer as she kicked at the retreating inmates.

"You ruined your own career you evil witch," Annie replied. "How could you let this happen?"

"Fuck you! Fuck you all! You're all a bunch of whores. Stupid worthless whores," shouted Jennifer.

"Someone patch up her ankle," said Annie.

"Any of you sluts touch me, I'll kick your fucking faces in," a heavily breathing and angry Jennifer shouted.

"Now we can't let you bleed to death. Besides you're our best evidence of the corruption at this prison," taunted Hannah Jane.

"Alright Hannah Jane, let's not get her any more riled up than she already is," jumped in Annie trying to gather herself after the fierce fight. "Jennifer, we have to stop the bleeding from your ankle. If we don't you could die. It looks pretty deep. So are you going to play nice so they can take care of you or do you want to die?"

"Okay, Okay," relented Jennifer.

"Good. Patch her up," said Annie as she walked off toward the conference room still rubbing her throat from the punches Jennifer gave to her earlier. Even though it hurt like hell she knew she was lucky because it could have been far worse if Jennifer had shot her. She thanked her lucky stars that she

would still have a chance to see her beautiful
daughter.

CHAPTER 61

Hearing more gunshots being fired inside the prison, the Incident Command Center was abuzz. James was still waiting patiently for a call from Russ Noblise. Before he could authorize any incursion of the SWAT teams and the Emergency Response Team, he needed the go ahead from Headquarters. But he realized that more people may be dying inside and that Jennifer may be involved. Sharon's phone rang.

"Sharon, we got a package for you," declared Annie.

"What is it?" asked Sharon.

"It's not a what but who."

"Well, who?"

"Associate Jennifer Welch."

"Jennifer is in there!" exclaimed Sharon. She

looked at James and repeated, "Jennifer is in there."

James looked disappointed as if he somehow already knew the answer and simply resumed typing on the laptop in front of him.

"She shot all those people we handed over to you guys earlier. We think she came to execute people who knew of her involvement in covering up the sexual abuse going on here at Mount Baker. Did any of them make it?"

"So far only Captain Draper but he is still touch-and-go. Is there any way you can prove she shot those four prison staff members?"

"Don't worry, she can't spin this. We have her on surveillance video firing a gun at several people."

"Okay. Now I think it's time you guys surrender the prison back to us."

"We haven't had a chance to hand over the video tapes to the U.S. Marshals or get our testimony recorded by the officials from the Office of the Attorney General as previously agreed."

"I know but..."

"But what. We had a deal."

"I know but the gunfire and with us not knowing what's going on in there caused us to call HQ for authorization to take action to save lives."

"Sharon, you got to work with us. I have a lot of ladies in here who are scared they'll be put squarely back in the same compromising position with prison staff forcing them or coercing them into performing sexual acts and retaliated against."

"I hear you Annie. I'll talk to the Incident Commander here and see what we can do."

"That's all I ask."

"I'll get back to you," Sharon said rather apprehensively. She knew it would only be a matter of time before Russ called back with decisive orders from the Governor's Office. Those orders may lead to more deaths inside the prison and she wanted to avoid that at all costs. After hanging up the phone, she walked toward James to brief him on the information she had gained from Annie.

CHAPTER 62

The nightly news began by showing Mount Baker Corrections Center for Women with a wide angle shot and then cut to Chuck Greenlee and Raquel Crisp who broke the story of the inmates. Both tried to maintain their journalistic objectivity, which became more difficult after viewing the video of Jessica Wick and several nights of reporting the story of these women including reporting on Annie's tenuous conviction for Murder in the Second Degree. Both Chuck and Raquel had been like most of us. Yeah, they all say they are innocent. However, reviewing Annie's trial and conviction led them to now understand that perhaps not every case was so clear cut.

Here was a woman who had gotten her ass kicked by a brute for two years. Now finally she lashed out in violence in return and the result was that the perpetrator wound up dead and a mother separated from her baby. Off-air they both talked about potentially how many other cases of people like Annie there were in our country of nearly three hundred million. Hell, how many other cases of wrongful conviction were out there because some witness misidentified the accused or the absolutely immune prosecutor overzealously prosecuted a case that was in the gray area between legal and illegal? These were all the things they discussed together and internally but now they were on the air and had a job to do.

"Good evening America. Welcome to the most trusted name in news. I'm Chuck Greenlee here with Raquel Crisp. Tonight at Mount Baker Corrections Center for Women in Bellingham there are reports of gunfire coming from inside the institution. The Department of Corrections' Communications Liaison at the scene reports that they have not identified the cause of the gunfire and cannot identify the names of anyone who may have been shot without notifying the next of kin first."

"Right Chuck, our video footage from a few minutes ago shows several ambulances leaving the scene of the hostage crisis at Mount Baker. Several are driving regular speeds with only one of them rushing with its lights and sirens blaring. Bellingham General Hospital will not release any information about who was brought in or what there condition is. We hope to get an update for you as soon as any news gets released," added Raquel as she and Chuck continued with the evening broadcast.

CHAPTER 63

Casey Draper had loved Doyle from the very first moment they met and he had lived up to her expectations by being a caring and loving husband. He always put her and the boys first. As a young CO at Mount Baker, Doyle didn't make much money as is common for the people who have one of the most dangerous jobs in America. But what he did make went to make sure the kids had clothes for school, food to eat, and a safe place to call home.

Doyle especially made sure that Casey could go to the hairdresser when she wanted even though she frequently avoided going to save money. For her, it was the little things that mattered most. Doyle would put a little bunch of violets in a vase outside of their bedroom door on special occasions like the anniversaries of the first time they kissed, the first time he said "I love you," and the first time she agreed to go on a date with him. He remembered all those little details that most men would never bother with remembering. He was special. Now all she could do was watch helplessly as he lay prone in the hospital bed on a ventilator. She waited for hours to hear from the specialists who were reviewing his medical charts and examining him.

The boys were rather strong in appearance. They felt a sense of responsibility for taking care of their mother. This responsibility came from the fact that on their various fishing trips with their father he frequently reminded them that one day he wouldn't be around to look after her and that that responsibility would fall on their shoulders. Here they were staring directly in the face of that responsibility and taking it on as was expected of them. Who knew how long they could keep it up? They were just boys.

Finally, the hospital's Chief of Surgery came into the room. He had a very serious yet concerned look on his face. As he approached the Drapers, they instinctively knew what was coming. "Mrs. Draper, the neurologists have completed their assessment of Mr. Draper. It appears that he has no high level brain activity. At the current rate, he has been comatose so long that the likelihood for a recovery is miniscule."

"What do you mean no high level brain activity?" asked Paul Draper.

"It means that he's not responding to our attempts to stimulate him or revive him. It means he has suffered an irreparable brain injury as a result of the extensive blood loss," responded the Chief of Surgery.

"What does that mean for us?" Casey queried.

"It means that you have a decision to make about continuing life support." That statement caused the entire family to begin crying uncontrollably. They had hoped for a miracle. That hope evaporated instantly upon hearing what the Chief of Surgery had to say.

"We can't do that," replied a tearful Casey. "We just can't."

"Mrs. Draper, I'm not asking for a decision to be made right away. I just want you to know where we stand with treatment options for Mr. Draper."

"Mom, you know dad wouldn't want to be like this. He told us. He wanted to be let go if he was a veg...a vegetable," cried John.

"I know but..."

"Mom, John's right. We have to do what dad asked us to do," added Paul.

"Okay, boys. We'll do what you father wanted. Doctor, please don't let him suffer anymore," Casey said.

"Do you want to get anyone down here? You know, other family members, priests, or somebody else," asked the Chief of Surgery.

"No, just us," responded Casey.

"Alright. Please take your time in saying goodbye to him." With that, the Chief of Surgery departed the room and began talking to the nurses at the nurses' station as the Drapers surrounded Doyle and began rubbing his hands and talking softly to him as they said their final goodbyes to him. Finally, Casey planted a soft and tender kiss on his lips.

CHAPTER 64

As news helicopters hovered overhead, the SWAT teams and Emergency Response Team were putting on their gear and getting into their armored vehicles. James looked on with apprehension after ordering the retaking of the prison from the inmates. Sharon stood next to James. Normally an unemotional woman, her eyes began to water but she quickly stifled the trickling dam of feelings. "So, I guess I can't call Annie back and warn her of what's coming?" Sharon asked.

"No, we can't tip them off. It might endanger the lives of the officers. I know how you feel though. It really seems like these women were justified in what they did," said James.

"Yeah, for sure. I just can't believe that Jennifer did something like this. I knew she was a member of the good old boys club that could do no wrong but letting this shit go on. This is ridiculous and reprehensible."

"I'm disappointed in Jennifer too. But right now we have to focus on the task at hand; ending this damn thing with the least amount of bloodshed possible. I don't want to see anyone else get hurt tonight. Nevertheless, I have to be realistic. It's very well likely we could see some of these ladies get killed." James and Sharon stood together and watched as the SWAT teams and the Emergency Response Team began driving to their designated entry points in the coordinated effort to retake the MBCCW.

CHAPTER 65

"Good evening America. Welcome to the most
trusted name in news. I'm Chuck Greenlee here with
Raquel Crisp. We interrupt your normal broadcast
because tonight there is increased activity outside of
the Mount Baker Corrections Center for Women. You
will recall that the female inmates at the prison rioted
and took control of the prison. Now, it appears that
SWAT teams from the Washington State Patrol, FBI,
and Whatcom County Sheriff's Office along with a
nearby prison's Emergency Response Team are
preparing to force their way into the institution and
put down the rebellion. The Governor has ordered the
Washington Army National Guard to cordon off the
roads surrounding the institution. We'll keep you
posted with the breaking news as it comes out.
Raquel."

"Thanks Chuck. Tonight we have with us
Siobhan Sunrise. Siobhan is the spokeswoman for the

protesters opposed to state officials being allowed to retake control of the women's prison for fear that the women will be subjected to the same rape and retaliation for speaking out. Hello Siobhan. What happened tonight at your protest site?"

"Hi Raquel, I just want to clarify that we're peace activists supporting the victims of sexual violence inside that prison. Anyways, we were singing songs, praying, and meditating when all of a sudden a State Patrol vehicle arrived and three patrolmen stepped out and told us we had to move because we were inside an area where they would be conducting operations and it was for our own safety that we leave."

"How did you respond to their request that you move?"

"It was more of an order rather than a request but we moved. We are peace activists. We're not there for violence."

"How many peace activists are out there?"

"There are about one-hundred and fifty of us."

"Are you aware that the operation the state patrolmen were speaking of was the retaking of the prison?"

"Yes, we just hope that no one gets hurt in this violent entrance into the prison. The law enforcement officers going into this prison have to realize that these women have been traumatized enough already. They should do their best not to further victimize these women with more violence. Our prayers are with the ladies of Mount Baker."

"Some people will argue that this is a prison and you can't just let the inmates run the institution so prison officials have to be put back in charge. What do you say to them?"

"We say we know that these ladies have violated the law and need to be held accountable for their criminal acts but raping them is not the way to do it. Neither is pointing guns at them as will be the case soon. After this is all said and done, we need to take a long and hard look at our prisons across the United States to determine if they're being operated in the most effective way. Or are we destroying these people. Most of these women will be getting out. Many of them have children. What good will they be to their children when they get released if they have been raped and tortured by prison staff. Will they get out and mimic this violent behavior in their interactions with their children and others? Will they get out and abuse drugs and alcohol again to push the memories of the trauma they suffered out of their minds? This is no different than when combat troops return from war after being involved in bloody battles and seeing friends and enemies bodies ripped to shreds. They often wash away those memories with drugs and alcohol."

"Soon the prison will be under the control of the state again, what is the next step for your group?"

"We'll continue to support these women every step of the way. We'll raise money for them to help them with getting counseling services, legal representation, whatever they need."

"Thank you for taking the time to do this interview with us tonight."

"Thank you Raquel for letting us get our message out there. We all have a responsibility to oppose all violence no matter who is engaging in it."

"Thank you Siobhan Sunrise."

As Chuck moved on to the next story in the nightly news lineup, Raquel smiled as she felt a swell of pride in her small role of helping promote an "anti-violence against women" message. She knew that every little effort counted.

CHAPTER 66

Annie stood up in the conference room after watching the surveillance cameras and seeing the SWAT teams and prison Emergency Response Team moving around at a rather high rate of speed. She knew that something was afoot. Now she had to think on the fly. She needed to come up with a plan to protect herself for Julia but also prevent the death of anymore of the women she had grown to care so much for during this ordeal. She had to convince them that their lives were important. She had to convince them to surrender.

"Ladies! Ladies, let's start the meeting. Now we have some serious decisions to make. First off, if you look at the surveillance cameras you see that something is happening outside. The last thing I want is for anything else to happen to you. You all have become like family to me. I really mean that from the bottom of my heart. Hannah Jane is like the big sister I never had," Annie said as she put an arm around Hannah Jane's shoulders and squeezed. "Patricia is like the overprotective aunt. All of you are my extended family. We wouldn't be where we are right now if it weren't for your efforts. But now I have a big request to make of you. We need to surrender. We need to surrender now. Outside, it's clear that the law enforcement officials are planning an assault on this prison to retake it. They won't be coming with rubber bullets. They'll be coming with real bullets because they know we have access to the prison's armory."

"But what about our plan to have our testimony taken by the lawyers from the Attorney General's Office?" asked Susan.

"Well, we're not going to be able to do that now. Associate Welch ruined our chances at that coming in here and shooting people," Annie replied.

"Yeah but we still have the video footage here to get to the U.S. Marshals also," Susan retorted. "They could destroy it all."

"I think that the videos are all safe now because we locked them inside the metal boxes the Marshals brought with them," responded Annie. "Besides the Marshals have a federal judge's court order to secure the videos. I don't think they'll let anyone stop them from securing them. Additionally, if any state officials interfere with the videos they face a contempt of court order that could land them in federal prison. It's time Susan. It's time for us to hand this place back over to the state."

"Annie's right Susan. We've accomplished a

great deal of our goals," Hannah Jane added.

"Now's the time ladies for us all to cell-in and await their arrival," said Annie. Looking around the room Annie could see that nearly all the women were in agreement as heads nodded and faces showed a general agreement with her comments except one. Susan from the Palouse Unit seemed to be upset. Without warning, Susan grabbed one of the guns from one of the inmates who had been on a security detail.

"I'm not going back into a cell. I've been in this prison for far too long. It's time for me to get the fuck out of here. You bitches aren't going to keep me locked up any longer," declared Susan. She was anxious and jittery. Susan had been convicted of a string of homicides involving johns who patronized her as a prostitute. After they had completed their sexual acts, she almost immediately stabbed them with a knife she kept hidden in an ankle holster. She was mentally ill but had been medicated for years while incarcerated at MBCCW. Now the medications had worn off and she was returning to her prior mental state.

"Susan you're going to jeopardize all of our lives here if you don't let us surrender," said Sibyl.

"I can't stand this being locked up shit. Are we going to let these motherfuckers keep raping us? Hell no. We're going to cut their fucking heads off," Susan said in an agitated voice.

"Put that goddamned gun down. You were never raped by any of these guys," added Patricia.

"It doesn't matter. We have to kill them for

what they did to Sibyl and Jessica and everybody else," replied Susan.

"Yeah but what if they kill us?" asked Annie.

"They can't kill us. We got guns," an irrational Susan said.

"We can't let you do this. None of us wants to die here today," said Annie.

"Then I'll just have to finish by myself," declared Susan as she started to pull the trigger and the women in the room began ducking in horror as yet another person set about their plan to murder.

CHAPTER 67

The State Patrol SWAT Team entered the Palouse Unit's main entrance. It was desolate, not a single person was seen. As the team moved cautiously down the hallway toward the first housing pod of the living unit, they noticed that there was a woman tied to a chair with a gag in her mouth and a note attached to her chest. The officers cautiously approached the woman and as they drew closer to her they could read the note which said "Mentally Ill, Need Meds."

Before quickly returning to their living units, the inmates subdued Susan only ten minutes prior to the SWAT team breaching the institution. She had begun pulling the trigger of the gun in an effort to shoot the women in the conference room of the Administration Building. However, the inmate who had the gun had unloaded it when it was issued to her because she didn't like guns and didn't want to hurt anyone. As soon as Annie realized that the gun was dry firing, she promptly moved toward Susan and punched her in the face knocking her to the ground. She then jumped on top of her and held her there until the others jumped in to help tie her up. Even once she was tied up, Susan continued yelling, cursing, and spitting at the others. So much so that they decided she needed to be gagged.

Leaving Susan tied to the chair, the officers moved ahead and gained entry to the first pod. Once inside they discovered something rather fascinating about this prison riot. All of the inmates had returned to their cells. Being cautious that it may be some kind of misdirection, the officers proceeded to move down each tier of the pod checking the cells to ensure they were locked. Only after being certain did the officers relax.

As the other teams moved into their assigned living units, they discovered the same scenario playing out. The Whatcom County Sheriff's SWAT Team found the Alpine Unit secure, the FBI SWAT Team found the Puget Unit secure, and the Emergency Response Team found the Columbia Unit secure. The inmates had all returned to their cells. There would be no one else losing their life in this prison uprising.

Annie and Sibyl stood inside their cell as the Emergency Response Team moved through the unit in a formation checking each cell. Annie felt satisfied that what they had accomplished in this insurgency had been a monumental fete. They had brought down one of the most corrupt prison administrations in the history of the United States. All she hoped for now was for vindication in a court of law; vindication for the women of Mount Baker in Judge O'Keefe's court room as well as for her own case, which was now up on appeal before the Washington Court of Appeals Division II based in Tacoma.

In the ensuing weeks and months, Annie received numerous visits from her mother and Julia. They were both able to stay in Bellingham for weeks on end as they received an overwhelming amount of donations from women's groups and individuals all over America. The public heard Annie's story through Sylvia. They heard about how she persevered in the face of having her mother turned away after several attempts to visit with Julia in retaliation for her recalcitrance in the face of the threats and attempts to extort sexual favors out of her.

Annie also received thousands of letters from all over the country from women who had empathized with her or had suffered their own domestic abuse tragedy. She wrote day and night trying to personally respond to every one of them. She had become somewhat of a national heroine. It's not often that a person who is imprisoned becomes a real-life folk hero. But Annie had become just that. While this was important to her, what was most important was that she was able to receive a promotion in her custody level allowing her to have contact visits with her mother and daughter. This was the icing on the cake. She was allowed to kiss and hug them. Especially Julia; with her she was able to reconnect with the baby girl who had stolen her heart. Annie was also unaware of a newly brewing controversy involving her.

CHAPTER 68

Two months after the riot ended, Dee Wilson, the jailer from Thurston County Jail, and Raquel Crisp stood on the steps of the Washington State Capitol Building holding megaphones. The day was blustery as the attendees stood dressed in heavy coats, gloves, and scarves clutching umbrellas in preparation of the usual Western Washington drizzle that was sure to eventually come. Dee and Raquel had met up when Raquel had been interviewing people about Annie's case. Dee had mentioned her interest in helping women who had suffered as a result of domestic violence but not knowing exactly what to do to help. A few more phone calls between the two of them followed and soon thereafter the "FREE ANNIE LONE" Campaign was born.

Now here the two of them stood before nearly two thousand women and men. Its goal was not legal. This campaign was not demanding the overturning of

Annie's conviction, which Sylvia was working on. It had a political goal. This campaign, started on an online social networking website with nearly one million people joining it, including about one hundred thousand in Washington, sought the pardoning of Annie. The group lobbied the Governor of Washington in an effort to pressure her to pardon Annie. The central basis for the argument was that Annie should never have been charged by the prosecutor or convicted by the jury.

Notwithstanding the fact that she was charged and convicted, the "FREE ANNIE LONE" Campaign didn't raise money or have a formal organization. It merely asked supporters to e-mail, call, fax, and mail the Governor of Washington. The idea being that if the pardoning powers of the Governor truly are political in nature and not legal then applying enough political pressure should force her into considering Annie's petition for a pardon. A petition filed not by Annie but by Dee Wilson and Raquel Crisp. Now Dee and Raquel knew very little about the process of obtaining a pardon but Raquel's boyfriend, a lawyer in Washington, D.C., did a mountain of research to assist the two in understanding the Governor's pardoning powers. They learned that the power had a long history in Anglo-American law.

The power of the pardon is an executive power historically held by the British Monarch in the English Common Law. The Crown held the power to forgive a person for his or her violation of the law. It was an entirely political power, which despite a person's conviction and sentencing under the law the Crown retained the power to wipe away that conviction.

With the passing of the British Monarchy in the former British North American colonies as a result of the American insurgency, the successor United States and its states assumed the powers that the Crown once possessed including the power of the pardon. As a result of the new country's adoption of federalism, the president of the United States holds the power to forgive individuals' violations of the federal law and the states' governors the power to forgive violations of state laws.

The Washington State Constitution recognizes the Governor's power to pardon in Article III, section 9 as prescribed by law. The Washington Legislature created the Clemency and Pardons Board in WASH. REV. CODE § 9.94A.885 to consider petitions for pardons, hold hearings on said petitions, and make recommendations to the Governor about those petitions. Avoiding the Board would be the quickest way to free Annie from Mount Baker Corrections Center for Women. The Board considered petitions for people who actually admitted their guilt and whether that person would be a contributing member of society if their pardon was granted and made recommendations to the Governor. Dee and Raquel believed that Annie was not guilty because she had a valid defense and should not have been charged or convicted so why should she go before a Board designed on guilt.

In discussing the issue with Raquel's boyfriend, the question arose as to whether they had to submit the petition to the Clemency and Pardons Board and whether the Governor could act independently of the Board and without the Board having considered the petition. The advice they received was yes on both questions. That was the gasoline that turned the smoldering fire both women felt on the issue of freeing Annie from prison into a raging inferno. What they once thought to be impossible seemed very possible. That is what landed Dee and Raquel both on the steps of the State Capitol on that day.

Lifting the megaphone to her lips, Dee sighed and started to speak but stumbled. She then pulled it together. "Thank you all for coming out today. We're here for one simple reason. To free Annie Lone!" A large cheer went up from the crowd. "We have a woman who stood up for herself, her daughter, and, without knowing it, all women's rights. We're not saying that violence is the answer but we are saying that you, no, we have the right to self-defense. We have the right not to be pushed, we have the right not to be choked, we have the right not to be punched, and we have the right not to be shot. Annie should not have been charged, tried, or convicted. Now it's up to us to standup for her; to standup for women all over America who may face prosecutorial overreaching. So let's standup to free Annie Lone!"

As the crowd roared to life, Dee stepped back and nodded to Raquel who lifted her megaphone. "Thank you all for being here today. In a few minutes, we're going to march to the Governor's Office. We're going to drop off the signed petitions showing the immense support we have gathered for her to exercise the gubernatorial pardon power. We're going to show the Governor that thousands of us want Annie pardoned and freed from prison today." The crowd came to life as hoots, hollers, and yells of approval rose up from its immense mass.

"Not simply because of her wrongful conviction but because of what she did for imprisoned women all over the United States. Sexual abuse of female inmates is no longer acceptable in America's jails and prisons. American families whose daughters, sisters, aunts, nieces, girlfriends, and wives make a mistake that land them in jail or prison are not there to serve the sexual desires of their jailers. They are there to account to society for their mistakes not to be coerced or forced to engage in sexual acts with jail and prison officials. I saw the video of Jessica Wick being raped and murdered by her jailers. It was horrific. The fact that these animals thought it necessary to record their crimes shows a general lack of fear of prosecution and, most importantly, a lack of humanity. But we're not going to stand by and let this continue. Are we?" The crowd responded with a thunderous "NO."

"If it weren't for Annie Lone, we wouldn't have known about this violent and evil group. We all have the right to know that our incarcerated loved ones aren't being sexually exploited. Now we have the opportunity to step up to the plate and play our part in making our jails and prisons safer. Just as Annie stood up for herself and the inmates of Mount Baker Corrections Center for Women, we need to stand up for all women housed in correctional facilities across this great land. The first step in doing so is freeing Annie Lone. Freeing her because of what she did for women at that prison and because she shouldn't have been incarcerated in the first place.

Before we go to see the Governor, we have a special guest we want to introduce to you. With us

today is Daryn Mallory. She is the mother of Annie
Lone and with her is little Julia Lone. The baby we've
all heard so much about." As Daryn stepped forward
holding Julia, she leaned toward the microphone.

"Thank you all for helping my daughter. This
means so much to me and it means so much to Annie."
With that Daryn stepped back. She was awed by the
sheer number of people that turned out to help her
daughter. Overwhelmed she began to cry as Dee and
Raquel rallied the supporters to begin the march to the
Governor's Office to deliver the petition. Over the
next several days the Governor was inundated with
requests from the tens of thousands of supporters of
Annie to free her. The opposing prosecutors and
others did step forward to attack the idea of a pardon
for a convicted killer, as they put it, but they were
disorganized and their message was drowned out by
the larger "FREE ANNIE LONE" Campaign.

CHAPTER 69

Annie and Sibyl returned to their cell from morning mainline and sat down to continue their conversation. James Toril, fresh off of his promotion to Lieutenant, approached Annie and Sibyl's cell. James received several commendations and awards from various organizations as a result of his handling of the prison riot. He even got to meet the Governor. In the two weeks following the end of the prison siege Annie's story received extensive media coverage but James also received some attention from media outlets. The media portrayed James as the one true honest public servant in a sea of criminal prison officials at Mount Baker Corrections Center for Women.

Despite the murders of Doyle Draper, Roy and Rachel Soren, and Lance Atron, Americans watched as Jennifer Welch and nearly a dozen other MBCCW officials took long perp-walks before television cameras as they were escorted into the Whatcom County Courthouse to face criminal charges. The criminal trials were watched closely by the state Office of the Attorney General and the U.S. Department of Justice. The former because it offered the Whatcom County Prosecuting Attorney's Office assistance where needed. The latter because it was considering filing federal criminal charges against the MBCCW suspects for violations of the inmates' civil rights, which was dependent upon the outcome of the state criminal trials. But as the verdicts of guilt were returned by juries in the criminal trials, federal prosecutors declined to seek grand jury indictments but the media attention on the operation of women's prisons from coast to coast intensified.

With all this bad news, the Washington Department of Corrections advanced James Toril as the trusted employee who effectively managed the crisis at the institution but, more importantly, stepped up to the plate by not trying to cover-up the criminal acts of his colleagues. He did interview after interview with the media promoting the notion that not everyone at MBCCW participated in the sexual abuse and assaults. He informed the media that if he had discovered the criminal enterprise within the prison he would have immediately informed the DOC officials at Headquarters and not been swayed by this so-called blue wall of silence that is so strong in so many uniformed criminal justice agencies across the country. After two weeks of interviews and working out of headquarters, James returned to MBCCW and began working in his new position as Lieutenant.

He was happy to be back at work, back in

Bellingham, back to his normal routine. Everything had quieted down at the prison with a return of normalcy except this morning. He got a telephone call at six in the morning at home from Russ Noblise with some very pressing news. That was why he approached Annie and Sibyl's cell this morning. He had urgent news to deliver. "Good morning, Lone," said James with a huge smile on his face.

"Good morning," replied Annie.

"Start getting your things together, the Governor signed a pardon this morning for you." He slid a collapsible box through the cell's bars for her.

"What?" she said excitedly.

"The Governor has pardoned you." Annie was overcome with emotion and immediately started crying. Sibyl went to her side and embraced her.

"I can't believe it. I'm getting out of here. I'm going to get to be with my baby everyday."

"You are. I should have mentioned this in the beginning but the pardon is conditional. The Governor wants to have you report to a Community Corrections Officer for one year after your release."

"I don't care. I just want to be home with Julia," Annie happily cried.

"Annie this is so great. You deserve this," Sibyl said as she hugged her friend.

"We have notified your attorney of the pardon and your immediate release from custody. She has arranged for someone to pick you up and get you to the airport," added Lieutenant James Toril.

"What about my mother? Has anyone told her?"

"Sylvia indicated that she would contact her to let her know of your release. Good luck with the rest of your life. You should be proud of what you did here Mrs. Lone; damned proud."

"Thank you Lieutenant Toril. Thank you so much."

"Don't thank me. Thank your supporters. They went to the mat for you." With that Lieutenant Toril walked away from the cell front smiling. He was relieved that Annie was being freed from prison. Annie started packing her personal property.

Annie hugged Sibyl again and looked her in the eye. "Sibyl, I couldn't have done this without you. I just want to thank you. You're the best friend that I've ever had. Damn it, you're the sister I wish I had."

"I feel the same way about you. Now stop crying. You go out there and take care of that little girl."

"When you get out of here, please come look me up."

A CO stepped toward the cell door. "Annie Lone, time to go."

Annie picked up her box of things and looked at

Sibyl one last time. "Take care of yourself Sibyl."

"You too Annie. You too."

The CO called to the control booth to open the cell door. Annie walked out for the last time and followed the CO down the tier toward the exit.

CHAPTER 70

As the taxi pulled up in front of the small rancher house on Danby Avenue in Olympia, Annie was anxious, anxious about where her life was headed, anxious about how prison had affected her, and how that would affect Julia. Then she remembered why she wanted to get away from Billy and why she fought so hard to get out of prison. She remembered that her life was dedicated to raising that baby girl. Julia needed her. She owed it to her. Feeling self-assured and confident, Annie opened the door of the taxi, handed the taxi driver twenty-five dollars, and stepped out.

As she walked up the path toward the front door, it suddenly swung open to reveal Daryn holding Julia. At that moment, Annie immediately burst into tears at the sight of them. She rushed toward the open door and embraced both of them. "I love you, Mom. I love you, Julia," Annie said kissing both of them on the cheek numerous times.

"Welcome home Annie. Welcome home," said Daryn.

Annie had dreamed about this moment. She had constantly played out the homecoming in her mind over and over again. But what she actually felt surpassed any dream she could have ever had. Over the next several weeks she spent nearly every waking moment with Julia and Daryn. They spent time at Percival Park letting Julia play on the playground, walked along Percival Landing looking at the boats moored nearby, and traversed the popular jogging path around Capitol Lake taking in the wonderful sea air blowing in from the nearby Budd Inlet. Annie stayed in touch with her friends at Mount Baker Corrections Center for Women. She wrote to Sibyl, Hannah Jane, and Patricia and even visited them once when Sylvia went to interview them in preparing their federal case.

As weeks turned to months, Annie had to be deposed in preparation for the case. The state assistant attorney general deposed her for more than three hours looking for inconsistencies in her story. But Annie's memory was flawless. She remembered every detail of what happened to her and what happened to her best friend Sibyl. The other women also held up in their own depositions substantially inhibiting the ability of the state to defend against the federal lawsuit.

With the class action certified and the case prepared for trial, the state asked Sylvia if her clients were willing to mediate the case. After discussing the case with the class representatives, Annie, Sibyl, Hannah Jane, and Carol, Sylvia mediated the case with the state but was unable to reach a settlement agreement. The state's last offer to the female inmates was three million dollars but didn't respond to any of the institutional changes proposed by the plaintiffs in the case. The state didn't want to negotiate any of the non-monetary relief that the class action suit sought. Some of the sought after changes included a confidential system for investigating inmate complaints about staff misconduct outside of the institution, offering counseling services to inmates when it was shown that the inmates were victims of staff sexual misconduct, and punishing anyone who retaliated against inmates who reported staff sexual misconduct.

The counseling services were extremely important because some of the inmate-victims were severely emotionally damaged by the things done to them. For example, Sibyl Enoch suffered terribly in the aftermath of her brutal rape. She poured her heart out to Annie in her letters. She revealed how she wanted to kill herself after what had happened to her. If it weren't for Annie being such a good friend, she wouldn't have made it. Annie showed her support by writing her often and visiting when she could. After discussing it with her mother, she even offered Sibyl a place to live when she released from the prison, which was accepted.

On the day of her release, Annie stood in the public access building awaiting Sibyl. As the controlled exit door swung open, Sibyl stepped out of the door wearing the clothing that she had on the day she was taken into the Thurston County Jail. She had on a pair of blue jeans and a pink tee shirt. In her hands, she held a plastic bag containing her personal belongings and an envelope with her gate money of $40. Both women wore gigantic smiles on their faces when they made eye contact. Their friendship had grown even stronger after Annie's release from MBCCW. They both felt the same love. The love that sister's have for one another when they grow up together. Annie never had a sister but Sibyl sure made her feel like she did. The two embraced each other and held it for an extended time before finally releasing it.

"Gosh it's so good to see you walk out that door. I've missed you so much," said Annie.

"It's so good to walk out of that door. I've missed you too and thank you for giving me a place to live," added Sibyl.

"I wouldn't have it any other way. We lived together all that time in that prison. Why wouldn't we live together now?"

"Sibyl you take care of yourself," said the CO. "Don't come back to this place."

"Believe me, I won't," replied Sibyl.

"What's the first thing you want to do?" asked Annie.

"I want to go get some ice cream. God, I've missed good ice cream."

"I'd like some ice cream too. I have my mom's car and we can go into Bellingham and find a place to get some."

"Well, what are we waiting for?" Annie and Sibyl exited the public entryway chatting each other up as if they had never been apart for the last several months. That's how it is with old friends. The friendship never dies.

Charles Malone

CHAPTER 71

The day of trial arrived for the federal lawsuit in front of Judge O'Keefe. Judge O'Keefe revealed to both parties the story of what happened to his sister giving them the chance to move for his recusal from the trial. However, neither party took him up on the opportunity. Jury selection lasted for about three days as Sylvia battled the Assistant Attorney General Imogene Alfredson. Imogene challenged nine young women in the jury pool in an effort to eliminate them from the jury.

Sylvia saw it as a shrewd move to get rid of potential jurors who may be understanding or sympathetic to plaintiffs since younger women tended to be less likely to blame the victim of rapes than older women. At least that was Sylvia's point of view, but Imogene argued that each woman knew someone personally who had been raped either forcibly or non-consensually while under the influence of alcohol or drugs and the women harbored bias toward suspected rapists, which could adversely affect the ability of the state to defend itself against this lawsuit. Finally, a jury of seven women and five men were impaneled.

As the trial started and the evidence began to be rolled out in front of the jury, the state knew almost immediately it was in trouble. Carol Platt was the first witness for the plaintiffs. There were six recorded videos that Carol hadn't previously seen or known of showing her having sexual relations with several different COs. She had always believed that she had been a willing participant in all of her sexual acts with COs at Mount Baker Corrections Center for Women but four of the six video recordings show her being coerced into sex acts that she was not initially willing to participate in including sex with eight COs at once in one video and being forced to consume several COs' semen in another video. In each of the videos, the COs chided Carol for her reluctance to perform the acts. One even suggested she would be placed in Segregation if she didn't cooperate. As Sylvia froze the video on a frame showing the younger Carol's face in a state of empty agony, the courtroom was filled with uncomfortable silence.

Watching the videos for the first time, Carol started crying rather uncontrollably, which triggered Sibyl and Annie's own tears as they looked on. Several members of the jury, even men, dabbed their eyes or blinked wildly in an effort not to cry. Carol realized that she had convinced herself that she had consented to the sex acts as a way to deal with the trauma of what had actually happened to her.

"Carol, do you remember any of this?" asked

Sylvia as she battled to hold back her own tears.

"I didn't at first," Carol responded.

"How do you forget something like that?"

"I...I guess I convinced myself that I wanted it. I guess I pushed it out of my mind. You know...what really happened."

"Do you remember what happened now?"

"Yes."

"Please tell the jury what really happened in the video where you are engaging in sexual acts with eight COs."

"In 1989, I was twenty-seven years old. I had only been in prison for about a year when I met CO Roger Reading. He's the 6'10" guy in the video. I fell in love with him from the instant I saw him."

"Did you know that you weren't supposed to have relationships with prison staff?"

"Of course I did. But he was charming and handsome. He convinced me that we could be together and not get caught. So I thought what the hell. Why not?"

"Did he do anything special for you?"

"Yes he did. Roger brought me candy, makeup, weed, pretty much whatever I wanted."

"When you say weed do you mean marijuana?"

"Yes."

"How long did this go on, you know, CO Reading bringing you gifts?"

"Probably about three or four weeks."

"Is this video the first time you and Roger were intimate?"

"No. We had performed oral sex on each other in a walk-in freezer."

"Could you describe what happened?"

"Well, we kissed each other. Roger told me he loved me. Then we gave each other oral sex. It was great."

"Why?"

"It was the first time a man truly showed any interest in me or so I thought. Before that guys thought of me as only a sex object. They wanted me to do it doggie style so they wouldn't have to look at me or kiss me or they only wanted me give them head but not return the favor."

"Was the video with the eight COs the first time you had intercourse with him?"

"Yes, it was going to be our first time."

"Did you know he was going to have his seven friends show up?"

"No. He surprised me when he showed up with them."

"Why did you go through with it?"

"Before the camera started rolling, he changed. He started calling me names and threatening me. Roger told me that I owed him. He told me he took a lot of risks to get those things, you know, the contraband, in to me. He told me that only he could protect me. Without his protection, any man in the institution could do whatever he wanted to me."

"So you felt like you had to do it?"

"Yes I did."

"Did you like what they did to you?"

"Look at my face. Do I look like I'm enjoying that?" Carol replied as she started tearing up again. As Sylvia continued her direct examination of Carol, the jury's attention remained riveted to her testimony including the revelation that Carol had poisoned and killed her husband to land herself behind bars for insurance money and setting fire to their home to make it look accidental under the influence of her controlling mother.

The state decided not to cross examine Carol because there was little they could do to attack her testimony. Sylvia had obtained a copy of a suicide note from Roger Reading's adult son. In it, he admitted to sex crimes at Mount Baker and not wanting to spend the rest of his life in prison. Carol admitted her role in the sexual acts that took place but the reality, as seen by the jurors, was that the prison staff should not have engaged in those acts with her.

In the following weeks, Annie took the stand where she discussed the late Doyle Draper's attempt to coerce her into having sex with him and the witnessed rape of her friend Sibyl. Her testimony went well. The jury clung to her every word. So many in the public had heard of her because of the orderly prison riot she led at MBCCW but refused to take all of the credit for organizing. She became something of a modern-day Joan of Arc. Everyone wanted to know more about her.

After stepping down from the witness stand, Annie returned to her private life with her mother and daughter in Olympia. Annie received dozens of interview requests with the mainstream media. She also received advice from an attorney in Sylvia's law firm to hire an agent once she began receiving offers for book deals. Heeding the advice, Annie was able to get a sizable advance for her story, which eventually led to a movie deal. This provided for her, her mother, and her baby Julia. Annie knew that her fifteen minutes might end soon and she had to move quickly to take advantage of the opportunities presented to her.

Back in Judge O'Keefe's courtroom the parties turned the case over to the jury with the wrapping up of closing arguments about the evidence. The jury deliberated for about three days before finally reaching its final verdict. In the courtroom of public opinion, no one doubted the result. The state of Washington would be held liable for what went on at MBCCW. The only open question would be how much the damages verdict would be and what equitable relief the judge would hand down.

"Alright, Mr. Foreman, has the jury reached a verdict?" asked Judge O'Keefe.

"Yes your honor," replied the Foreman.

"Bailiff, bring me the verdict form," directed Judge O'Keefe. Once the bailiff had retrieved and delivered the verdict form from the Foreman, Judge O'Keefe looked it over thoroughly as the federal courtroom was filled with a nervous silence.

"Everything looks to be in order," said the judge as he clutched the verdict form firmly. As Judge O'Keefe proceeded to read the verdict form questions and the jury's response to those questions it became readily apparent that all of the individually named defendants including Associate Superintendent Jennifer Welch and Doyle Draper's estate were found liable for violating the inmates' Eighth Amendment rights to be free from Cruel and Unusual Punishment for the systematic program of rape, torture, and murder. The jury also found several of them liable under the state law for assault, battery, false imprisonment, conversion, and trespasses to chattels.

The jury also found the state of Washington liable for negligent supervision and retention of its employees for their tortious conduct committed against the female inmates under state law. The jury ordered the state to pay the injured inmates in the class action lawsuit $15,000,000 in economic damages for the past and future medical and mental health costs that the inmates would need as well as the lost earning capacity of those like Jessica Wick. The state was also ordered to pay $30,000,000 in non-economic damages based on the pain and suffering of the women who endured the agony and humiliation of the rapes like Carol Plat.

The individually named defendants didn't escape the jury's dishing out of justice. In fact, it hammered Jennifer Welch the most. She was ordered to pay $3,000,000 in economic damages, $3,000,000 in non-economic damages, and $3,000,000 in punitive damages. The punitive damages awarded by the jury were intended to punish Jennifer for her involvement in, and covering up of, the sex ring that she would be personally responsible for paying. All in all, the jury awarded nearly $95,000,000 in total damages to the female inmates in the class action lawsuit.

The media headlines were absolutely unforgiving to the state Department of Corrections. The 24-hour news cycle focused on key pieces of evidence exposed during the trial that appeared to implicate the highest executive officials within the Department. One piece of exposed evidence came during the cross examination of the Superintendent Sarah Loons by Sylvia in which it was shown that Corrections Secretary Bob James pressured her into appointing Jennifer Welch as her Associate Superintendent despite Sarah's misgivings about doing so. As a result, the Governor asked for the resignation of the Corrections Secretary. Sarah, nationally known for her involvement in prison reforms, was elevated to the position of Corrections Secretary.

The door to Annie's bedroom swung open as fourteen-month old Julia bounded across the floor toward her mother lying in bed watching the morning news coverage. As Sarah Loons began shaking the Governor's hand, Annie turned the television off. She grabbed the little girl and pulled her into bed with her and gave her a big kiss. "Good morning, sweetie. Did you have a goodnight?" Not answering her mother, Julia pointed out the window as the sun blindingly peaked through the bedroom window to welcome the start of a new day.

CHAPTER 72: EPILOGUE

Paul ran along the path surrounding Capitol Lake at about 6 a.m. on this rather chilly spring morning. He loved taking in the scene of the huge variety of seabirds that visited the lake regularly. Everything from the rebounding brown pelican to the occasional crane could be seen bathing and feeding in the waters of the lake. As Paul reached the end of his run, he started walking back toward his car parked in the lot of Percival Park where the boats where docked behind the Shellfish House. Paul crossed Fifth and Fourth Avenue to start the walk along Percival Landing where he could look at the boats docked nearby in calm waters as he cooled down.

Remembering how clear the sky was he looked northwest out over the water and saw an extremely beautiful sight. The snow covered peaks of the Olympic Mountains. Paul thought to himself this is why he moved here from Georgia. This has got to be the most beautiful place in America, if not the world. Yes, it rained plenty here but when the sun came out Western Washington was absolutely stunning. Paul's quick gait slowed as he continued on toward his car. As he reached the parking lot he heard a sound coming from near the little blue building that held the men and women's restrooms. The sound reminded Paul of a wounded animal.

He stopped walking and started listening carefully to the sound to see where it was coming from. Realizing it was coming from behind the building, Paul slowly walked toward it to investigate. The closer Paul got to the sound the more he realized it was a loud whimper that he heard. Reaching the corner of the building, Paul peeped around it to see what was going on. He saw a woman sitting on the ground in a semi-fetal position. She was dressed in the standard fitness attire except that she held her shorts in her hand.

"Are you okay?" Paul asked. The woman immediately began screaming hysterically. A startled Paul jumped backward and reached for his cell phone to dial 911.

"911, how may I assist you?" asked the operator.

"I just found a woman down here on Percival Landing behind the bathrooms. I think she needs some help."

"Is that her screaming?"

"Yes. She won't stop."

"The police and an ambulance are on the way. Is she bleeding?"

"No."

"Do you know her?"

"No."

With the screaming unsettling her, the operator asked, "Are you sure she's not hurt in any way?"

"No, I'm not sure. I do see the word DEREGULATE scrawled across her forehead and some other writing on her arms and legs but I can't make it out."

"I see a police cruiser coming down Columbia toward me."

"Okay sir. You can hang up to talk to the officers when they arrive."

As the police cruiser pulled into the parking lot, the male officer stepped out and immediately radioed for the assistance of a female officer. The woman's screaming stopped at the sight of the police car. The ambulance arrived about thirty seconds later. The EMTs realized that the woman may be the victim of a sexual assault so the male EMT stood back as the female EMT assessed the woman's injuries.

ABOUT THE AUTHOR

Charles enjoys writing suspense stories about strong
women overcoming tough odds. This is his debut novel.
Charles is an adjunct professor at Pierce College where
he teaches Business Law and Introduction to Law as well
as works for the Washington State Department of
Corrections. Charles is a graduate of Western
Washington University and Willamette University
College of Law. Charles currently resides in the beautiful
Evergreen State with his family.